Praise for Cold F

'Fun, sexy and fabulously festive...I enjoyed every minute of it.'
Bestselling author Jane Costello

'A real feel-good book that had me smiling, purring and laughing in equal measure'
Becca's Books

'It is without a doubt one of the best Christmas reads I've ever read...It is fabulous!'
The Book Geek Wears Pyjamas

'A fun and flirty Christmas romance with plenty of steamy moments, this book is anything but cold.'
Book Chick City

'This is the most wonderful Christmas novel to curl up with during the cold months. I loved it.'
Girls Love To Read

'Currently holding a spot in my heart for favourite Chick Lit heroine of the year (possibly of all time…).'
Chick Lit Love

DEBBIE JOHNSON

After spending many years working as a journalist, I decided to stop telling other people's stories, and start making up my own! I work from home in a very messy house near the beach, and write in between pouring bowls of Coco Pops for my three children and my dog (only kidding – he prefers Frosties!). I'm married to a man who is both a librarian and a musician – the perfect combination – and love to write pure, escapist fun. As well as romance, I'm also a published author in fantasy, and am working hard on crime as well. Or writing about it, at least.

http://www.debbiejohnsonauthor.com/

@debbiemjohnson

Pippa's Cornish Dream

Debbie Johnson

Harper*Impulse* an imprint of
HarperCollins*Publishers* Ltd
1 London Bridge Street
London SE1 9GF

www.harpercollins.co.uk

A Paperback Original 2015

First published in Great Britain in ebook format by Harper*Impulse* 2015

A catalogue record for this book is
available from the British Library

ISBN: 9780008150501

Automatically produced by Atomik ePublisher from Easypress

Chapter 1

"Looking hot today, babe," Pippa Harte said out loud as she caught a glimpse of herself in the bathroom mirror.

If, she thought ruefully, your definition of "hot" ran to electric-shock hair dragged back into an elastic band, smudges of oil as blusher and WD40 as perfume. Not to mention the glamorous accessories – elbow-length green rubber gloves, fresh from the Paris catwalk. Ooh la la!

In her hand she was wielding a toilet brush, the bristles wrapped in a plastic carrier bag from the local supermarket, the handles tied in a dangling bow around the pole.

"Well, here goes nothing..." she muttered, gazing down into the bowl of the loo. The very blocked bowl of the loo. The water was already up to the rim and one more flush was likely to send it over the edge. She'd been there before and knew that this one bit of dodgy plumbing was capable of recreating scenes from the Titanic.

Not, she thought, this time. This time, she would triumph – using her scientific know-how to defeat the Evil Bog of Destiny. She plunged the toilet brush in, shoved it hard and as far into the U-bend as she could. Create a vacuum, she recited in her head, then nature will fill it...

She sent up a quick prayer to the Patron Saint of Holiday Home Owners and tugged the flush handle, simultaneously pulling the wrapped brush out with a flourish. She stood back, prepared to jump aside if the floodgates opened, and looked on with something akin to joy as the water ebbed, flowed and swirled – all the way down the pipes!

"Yay!" she shouted, doing a victory jig around the room and out into the landing of Honeysuckle Cottage, "I did it! I am woman! I created a vacuum! Yay! Thank you YouTube!"

She was so happy, she managed to ignore two things – the tiny drops of toilet water flying from the plastic bag as she danced, and the man who had been standing outside in the hallway watching her. She jigged her way smack bang into him and dropped the brush in shock. It landed with a soggy, plastic plop on his expensive-looking walking boots. Oops!

"Oh!" she said, jumping back in surprise. "I'm so sorry...don't worry, it was clean water..." she added, using her wellies to toe the offending item away. "Not like last time...that was, well. Yuk. You probably don't want to know..."

She looked up, a wide grin cracking her oil-smudged face – nothing could bring her down, she decided, not after that minor miracle. And really, nothing she was looking at could dissuade her that the patron saint hadn't been listening after all – he was gorgeous. Six-two or thereabouts; broad shoulders packed up in a khaki-green Berghaus; long legs in denim; and the deepest, darkest brown eyes she'd ever seen on a human. Really, even the dairy cows she knew up close and personal couldn't compete. A wide mouth, kissable lips and dark, longish hair drifting over tanned, outdoorsy skin, damp from the drizzle outside. Or possibly the toilet brush, she thought with a twinge of guilt. Welcome to Cornwall.

"Are you Mr Retallick?" she asked, knowing the names of all her guests in advance. This one was early, but she wouldn't let that sour her mood. Not when the gods of the toilet had smiled upon her so warmly.

"I am – I hope it's okay to be here a few hours ahead of schedule? You seemed to be having some kind of rave..." he said, gesturing into the bathroom. His voice was deep and sounded like chocolate would if it could talk.

"Yes, that's what we do for fun around here, bathroom raving – the more the merrier, Mr Retallick, feel free to join in!"

She rubbed her face, realising that using a flirtatious tone with a handsome stranger might work better if she didn't look like a teenage grease monkey. The dungarees she wore were practical when she was doing her jobs around the farm, but it wasn't what you'd call chic. Mr Retallick – Ben, if she remembered rightly – looked like money. And style. And sex. He wouldn't look twice at a girl like her, even if she did have world-class DIY skills.

"I was just celebrating," she added. "I used my superior intellect to defeat the evil toilet, you see."

"You're celebrating the fact that you have a superior intellect to a toilet?" he asked, shrugging off his backpack and raising an amused eyebrow.

"Well, us country girls have to take our victories where we can find them, Mr Retallick...Retallick...that's a local name, isn't it?" she asked. It didn't seem likely that anyone from North Cornwall was coming on holiday to North Cornwall, but stranger things had happened. Maybe his wife had kicked him out, she thought, glancing surreptitiously at his ring finger. His bare ring finger. Not that she cared.

"Yes, I had family here once," he answered. "Long gone now."

He was perfectly polite, but something in his voice told her to back off. That was fine by her – she knew enough about families to understand that they were complicated. Her own, for example, was so weird you could make a sitcom about it. A lot of people came to Harte Farm for privacy, peace, seclusion. Which was a good job, as it was perched on top of a windswept hill overlooking the crashing waves of the Atlantic Ocean – not the place for a buzzing social life. If Mr Retallick wanted to be left alone, she would respect that. Even if he was the hottest thing in hotsville.

"How's it going in there?" he asked, gesturing towards the bathroom, where her various tools lay scattered on the harlequin-tiled floor. Not the best of first impressions, she thought, gathering them all back up and stowing them in her dad's old metal box. But then again, that's what you got when you turned up two hours before check-in. Behind the exterior of every chocolate-box-perfect holiday cottage lies a potential plumbing disaster – one she couldn't afford to pay a professional to deal with.

"Fine and dandy, I assure you," she replied, wiping her oil-smeared hands down on her dungarees.

"I'm Pippa Harte, welcome to our farm," she said. "I'd offer you my hand but – "

"I don't know where it's been?" he finished, his face deadpan but his tone amused. He was one of those chaps, she thought. Not one for belly laughs and grin-fests, but dry and witty. She liked those chaps. Or she used to, back in the day when she had anything to do with chaps at all.

"Well, I think you know exactly where it's been – that's the problem! You're staying for a week aren't you, Mr Retallick? Lovely weather you have for it!"

As the skies had been lashing a steady drizzle for the last two days, slanted almost horizontal by the gale-force winds, she was obviously joking. A lot of guests would have complained – city types in particular seemed to think the countryside should come with guaranteed sunshine whenever they visited – but he just shrugged those actually-now-you-mention-it-pretty-awesome shoulders and made a "them's the breaks" comment.

Pippa stared at him as he unzipped his coat, wondering if they'd met before. It wasn't just the Cornish name – it was the face. The eyes in particular. They were pretty spectacular eyes, after all, and she had the uncanny feeling she'd looked into them before.

"Have we met?" she asked. "You look really familiar..."

His face changed as fast as a storm raging in from the sea, the already dark eyes shading even deeper, a frown marring the skin of his fine, strong forehead. She felt a rebuff coming on and prepared to handle it. She'd been running this holiday business practically single-handed for three years now and had learned to deal with all kinds of strange visitors and their foibles.

As he opened his mouth to speak, the front door flew open and Daisy ran in, blonde curls swirling in a wild, tangled halo around her face. Predictably enough Lily followed, hot on her heels and just as flustered.

Daisy screeched, "SpongeBob's escaped again! She's –" "– pooing all over the courtyard!" finished Lily. They were identical twins, nine years old, and never seemed to be able to complete a sentence without each other's help. Which was at least an improvement on the secret language they'd used exclusively until they were seven. Pippa had been on the verge of calling in an exorcist when they suddenly stopped, although she still occasionally heard them gibbering together at night in their bedroom. Still, as long as their heads weren't spinning round, she was happy.

"Oh...sausages!" said Pippa, vaulting over Mr Retallick's rucksack and sprinting out and around the back to the courtyard. Sure enough, there was SpongeBob – that's what happens when you let kids name cows – munching away on the hydrangeas. She looked up as Pippa approached, her wide mouth sliding slowly from side to side as she chewed, her long-lashed eyes placid. At least to the untrained eye. Pippa had tangled with SpongeBob one too many times to be tricked.

"Daisy, Lily! One to the left, one to the right!" she shouted. "Scotty – I know you're out there somewhere – get the gate open!"

On cue, a little boy of about four, with the same long, wild blonde hair, appeared from behind the decorative water trough and ran over to a broad metal gate, reaching up on tiptoes to unhook the blue nylon string that tied it closed.

Pippa advanced steadily, hopping over the steaming gifts that SpongeBob had deposited on the cobbles, muttering the fake swear words she used in front of the kids – variations of "sugar", "broomsticks", "rubber ducks" and her personal favourite, "molluscs!" She noticed Mr Retallick coming closer from the corner of her eye and shouted out to him, "Don't be fooled! I know she looks like a pin-up, but this is the Osama bin Laden of cows! Best stay away!"

He nodded and instead headed towards the metal feed bucket that had been abandoned next to the gate. He picked it up and banged it with his fist so the contents rattled. SpongeBob looked up and over, her broad head turning towards the noise. Her eyes narrowed – Pippa swore they did – as she thought about it. Weighed up the pros and cons in her big cow brain.

Mr Retallick shook the feed bucket some more and walked through the gate towards the barn. Pippa walked closer to the cow, making gentle shooing gestures with her hands. Daisy and Lily edged in nearer on either side and Pippa could see their tiny blonde heads reflected in SpongeBob's huge, liquid brown pupils. They patted her on the side and Pippa gave a delicate shove from the rear, careful to avoid clomping hooves and swishing tails that could catch you in the eye if the animal got her dander up.

Finally, the combination of carrot and stick worked and she lumbered slowly towards the gate, after one final defiant munch of bright-purple hydrangea petals. She still had one dangling from her mouth as she walked.

"Into the barn!" shouted Pippa, watching as her early guest nodded and strode forward, angling long legs over the muddy puddles, leading the evil cow genius right inside. He smacked her on the behind as she wandered through and SpongeBob turned to give him the evil-cow genius eye. He gave her the eye back before shutting and latching the barn door.

Then he stood, hands on hips, threw his head back and laughed. Laughed long and hard, and loud. Pippa looked on in fascination, drinking in the sight of this stunning male specimen standing in her farmyard in the rain. Drizzle dripped from his soaked hair, over his forehead, along the slightly aquiline ridge of his nose, down to the sensual curve of his wide mouth. He really was drop-dead gorgeous. And even better, seemed to know his way around a cow. Wow! The perfect man. Now, if he could iron school uniforms and turn into a pizza after sex, even better.

The children scurried closer, looking at him with similar curiosity, Scotty clutching onto her hand for security. The twins were fearless, but her baby? He always needed an extra layer of security. Which was fine by her – as long as he still wasn't climbing into bed for cuddles when he was 16, she would always be available for hand-holding. She gave his fingers a little squeeze of reassurance.

"Thank you, Mr Retallick," she said. " I see you've spent some time in the company of cows before?"

"There are many answers to that, Miss Harte, but I'll restrain myself – and it was my pleasure. Been a while since I was at the business end of a Friesian. This used to be a dairy farm, didn't it?"

"Yes. 500 head. But my parents...aren't here any more. It's just us. So we converted to holiday lets. A working farm is – well, a lot of work. Too much for this gang of troublemakers, anyway."

"By 'us', you mean..." he cast his spookily sexy brown eyes over the gathered crowd, which now numbered Pippa, Daisy, Lily, Scotty, a nanny goat called Ben Ten and a pair of Muscovy ducks known as Phineas and Ferb. In fact, Pippa thought, there was only one person missing. As usual.

"Yes. Us. These are my brothers and sisters, and our animal friends," she said, introducing them all individually. "And there's one missing. Patrick. He's seventeen, and he'll be the one hiding somewhere after leaving the barn door open."

"Again!" said Lily and Daisy in unison, rolling their eyes in a way that spoke volumes about Patrick and his various misdemeanours.

"You look after all of...*these*?" said Ben Retallick, frowning as he looked at this slip of a girl, smudged in oil, crazy blonde hair escaping in corkscrew tufts from an elastic band, soaking wet in her torn dungarees.

He couldn't quite believe that she was playing mother hen to this whole brood. She only looked about eighteen herself, which had been giving him some major fits of the guilts since he'd arrived. The minute he'd seen her leaning over that broken lav, pert butt in the air, he'd noticed the fact she wore nothing but a tatty hot-pink t-shirt beneath those dungarees. He'd been working very hard not to notice how tight it was – or the fact that she didn't have a bra on – ever since. It had been difficult to know where to look. He had enough self-loathing going on as it was, without adding perving over a teenager to the list. And now it seemed he'd been wrong – she must be a bit older than that, surely, to have all this responsibility resting on those slender shoulders?

"Yes, Mr Retallick," she said firmly, drawing herself up to her full height – which had to be all of five foot three in her ancient Hunter wellies – and fixing him with kind of withering look clearly intended to make parts of him shrivel up and die. "I do indeed look after all of...*these*. We live together in an old shoe on top of the hill. Now, thanks for your help, and feel free to take yourself right back to Honeysuckle and settle in."

Her tone had changed – the easy humour and casual flirtation of earlier had disappeared – and instead she sounded wary, formal.

Mightily huffy, in fact. He'd upset her without even trying – a specialist subject of his. He felt a shiver run through him: not fear, not quite, but a spark of something...admiration, he thought. That was it. This tiny woman, almost a child from the looks of it, was swollen up with pride and fury and protective instinct. He'd poked a stick at her family, and now she was preparing to shove it right where the sun doesn't shine. Which, he thought, looking around him at the familiar farmyard, was pretty much everywhere in Cornwall right now.

"Right. I'll do just that," he said. "See you around, Pippa. Daisy. Lily. Scotty. Ben Ten. Phineas and Ferb. Give my regards to Madame SpongeBob."

He nodded at each of them individually as he turned to walk away, and Pippa felt her anger soften down to mild irritation. He'd remembered all of their names. Even the animals. That was pretty much a first in her experience; even she forgot them sometimes, resorting to "You, there, with the feathers!", or "Oi! Boy child!"

Maybe he wasn't that bad after all, she thought. Possibly he was just one of those unintentionally rude people who doesn't realise they're being offensive. Or possibly, she admitted, she was just one of those unintentionally prickly people who don't realise they're being defensive. She'd had a lot to defend over the years, and when it came to the kids and her ability to care for them, defensive was her default setting. None of which was tall, dark and cow-handy's fault.

She chased after him as he strode away, wellies squelching in the mud.

"Wait!" she shouted, tugging hold of his arm to stop him. "Where do I know you from, really? You're so familiar..." she said, realising as she touched it that his arm was solid as the oaks shading the side of the farm driveway. He looked city, but he felt country. He felt good.

The shutters went down again and he glanced at her clinging hand, raising his eyebrow eloquently: Back Off, Broomstick, clear as day.

Ben sighed, watched as her hand peeled away from his arm. She was the same as all the rest. Just another stranger who felt she knew him. Not quite there yet, still piecing it together, but give it a few minutes – she'd match the face with the name, with the story, with the legend. And she'd assume she knew him inside out. They all did.

He felt the familiar sense of frustration rise within him. It had been over a year since his release from prison, but still people stopped him. Still people chatted to him, touched him without permission, slapped him on the back and tried to shake his hand. Congratulated him, told him well done, like he was a hero for having survived eight months in HMP Scorton. He hated it. The lack of privacy, the pictures in the paper, the feeling of having his whole life played out in public. In fact, he'd come here to try and escape exactly that – back here to this isolated stretch of Cornish coastline, where the cows outnumbered the people and the internet was patchy at best. He'd hoped to have a week of solitude, without any prying eyes or being expected to bare his soul to complete strangers. Which showed what he knew – even here, his face was known.

Pippa stared at him intently, rubbing her cheeks and smudging that oil patch even harder into the milky-smooth velvet of her skin. Huge, cornflower-blue eyes. English rose all the way, if English roses had taken to abandoning the need for underwear and had just trodden in a cow pat.

He waited the few beats he knew it would take, saw the confusion in her eyes clear as she finally recognised him. Never mind, he thought. He could leave in the night; find somewhere even more deserted. Somewhere his face wouldn't be known. Somewhere they wouldn't have him pegged as the UK's most popular jailbird. Somewhere he wouldn't have to face someone who thought they knew him, thought they understood his story.

She pointed one grimy finger at him, and said, triumphantly: "You! I've figured it out! I know who you are! You're that bastard who threw me in the duckpond when I was seven!"

Chapter 2

Ben stared back at her, wondering if he'd fallen into some kind of wormhole and landed in an alternative reality. Okay. She did recognise him – but not for the reasons he'd assumed. She hadn't got a clue who Ben Retallick really was, had never heard of his case, never heard of Darren McConnell, and clearly hadn't got any idea that he was one of the most famous criminals in the country. He'd assumed she would be like all the rest – about to quiz him, prod him, look at him with that familiar mix of admiration and fear.

Well... she hadn't. She seemed to have him pegged for a far more historic crime – one he couldn't even remember. Maybe he'd started to believe his own hype...

"It was a long time ago – fourteen years or something like it – but I know it was you, there's no point denying it!" she said, almost jumping up and down in her excitement. Again, he studiously avoided looking at her upper half. She might be twenty-one, if he had the maths right there, but it was still a decade or so younger than him. It was still...wrong. And he'd worked very hard at avoiding women altogether since he'd been released. Since Johanna and her family made it clear they wanted nothing to do with a common-or-garden ex-con, no matter how justified his actions had been. Johanna – his fiancée when the incident that changed his life forever had occurred – had disappeared as fast as his career. She was engaged again now, he heard, to some corporate lawyer in Abu Dhabi. Good luck to her. And him, poor bastard – he'd need it.

"I'm sorry, but I'm not entirely sure what you're talking about," he replied, ragging himself back to the here, the now, and to Pippa – wondering if she'd accidentally sniffed some adhesive while she was fixing the loo.

She poked him in the chest with one finger – hard enough that it made him take a step back.

"You remember! Of course you do! It was ages ago, and you were here with your...grandfather, I think? Is that right? He was talking to my dad about some business thing or another, and you stayed here for a couple of nights. I was seven, so Patrick would have been, well, about three, and the twins and Scotty didn't even exist then. You seemed really glamorous, all the way from London – don't you remember, really?"

She gazed up at him expectantly, eyes huge and sparkling, and he realised he didn't want to disappoint her, didn't want to dismiss what was clearly still vivid in her mind – but he genuinely couldn't remember.

"I know I came here," he said, screwing his eyes up in concentration. "It's one of the reasons I booked my stay. I was eighteen, I think, spending the summer with my granddad before I went off to uni. I was bored rigid. There were...yes, there were some kids, I remember now!"

He cast his mind back: eighteen. Jesus. A whole lifetime ago. His parents had just moved to Australia and he was packed off to his granddad for a few months, filling in time until he started his law degree.

It was a different world back then. A world of youthful arrogance and easy potential and the safe and certain knowledge that the whole universe was his for the taking. An endless summer of heat and rain and surfing; blonde-haired girls with skin that tasted of saltwater; of working on his grandfather's farm and drinking cider and planning the rest of his life. His granddad, a wizened old man with a leanly corded body even in his seventies, had brought him to Harte Farm to discuss a joint venture with the vaguely hippy-ish couple who owned it. They were organic, he thought – ahead of their time.

And there were kids, yes, now he thought about it. A sulky brat of a boy, who had a habit of hiding and spying, and a hooligan girl with wild hair and a tendency to walk around naked. He looked at Pippa again. At the windswept tresses, roughly tied up into a boisterous ponytail. At the braless chest beneath the hot-pink jersey.

Really? Could that be her? All grown up, in ways you can never imagine when they're seven and you're eighteen? When that feels like a world of difference, the unthinkable rather than the inadvisable?

"You jumped on my head," he said, smiling at the memory. He saw it now: he'd had a hangover, as was usual back then. Too much scrumpy the night before. He'd been trying to sleep it off in the fields, found a patch of shade beneath the spreading arms of one of the old oaks that dotted the place. Half asleep, dreaming of London and home and those sailing girls with the salty skin and dirty laughs.

She'd yelled, like Boadicea screaming out a war cry, and launched herself from the lower branches of the tree, landing straight on top of him. He'd never even noticed her – she'd been wearing camouflage paint, greened-up like Rambo, hiding in the dappled leaves. Twigs stuck in her hair, soles of her bare feet covered in mud from running wild all day.

It amused him to think of it now, but he'd been a bit embarrassed at the time. Shocked out of his stupor by Stig of the Dump, caught out by a kid. A strange and slightly scary kid, who seemed to have made him the target of some kind of farm-based war game. God knows how long she'd been up there, watching him as he snored and drooled and sweated cider.

He'd picked her up by the skinny ankles and run all the way across the field, dangling her inches from the ground. She screamed and yelled and twisted herself up to try and scratch him, but he held firm until he reached the duck pond – where he'd swung her back and forth as if he was winding up for the Olympic discus, then let her fly through the air and land with a huge splash in the middle of the water.

His grandfather had given him a right telling off – what if she couldn't swim? What if she'd banged her head? What if she'd squashed a duck? But her parents, they'd been cool. Just laughed and said it served her right – she was a little savage and deserved a bit of her own medicine. Yeah, they'd been cool, and from what she said a few minutes ago, they were gone now. They might have taken off for a commune in Marrakesh, but he got the impression that wasn't what she'd meant. Rather that they were dead, like his grandfather. That the little girl he remembered had had to grow up very quickly, and way too soon.

"You remember now, don't you?" she asked, laughing. "You remember my war cry?"

She let it out again and he heard Scotty, Lily and Daisy join in in the background. My God! A whole family of them! Savages, one and all.

"Okay, okay...I surrender!" he said, holding up his hands in the universal gesture of giving up. "I do remember now – but you can't blame me for not recognising you. You have changed a bit, you know? You're more..."

He floundered, trying to find a word that didn't sound lecherous, curling fingers against his palm in case they accidentally made the equally universal gesture for "curvy-woman shaped".

"Yes?" she said, hitching an eyebrow up at him suggestively. "More what, precisely?"

He looked awkward, less self-assured and arrogant. The tiny lines at the corners of his eyes crinkled up, showing white beneath his healthy outdoorsy tan. She'd had a terrible crush on him back then, Pippa remembered. He'd been this tall, handsome, exotic stranger and she used to sneak around following him. Obviously, she barely registered on his all-grown-up radar. The scream-and-jump routine had just been her way of getting his attention. Her pick-up techniques had improved...well, not significantly since then, she acknowledged. It's not like she'd had much practice.

"Just...more," he said, finally, gazing over her shoulder as though he was trying to avoid making eye contact with her. "Who's that?" he asked, chocolate-drop eyes narrowing.

"What? Who?" blathered Pippa, who'd been slightly lost in thought as she looked up at his face. How could she not have remembered him straight away? He'd been the first love of her life, and had broken her tiny heart by dunking her in the duck pond – which, she had to admit, she thoroughly deserved.

She turned, following his gaze. Saw a plume of black smoke, then heard the bang. The scrape. The crash and grind of metal clashing on the gravel.

"Oh," she said, the fun fading from her cornflower eyes, "that. That's Patrick. On his bike. Or off it, perhaps."

"Has he...just crashed it? Is he all right?" said Ben, watching as the gunmetal smoke funnelled up into the equally grey sky. This was all a bit surreal, as though he'd wandered into an episode of the *Twilight Zone*. And he'd thought his life was odd.

"Yes, he's just crashed it," she replied, setting off at a fast clip towards the scene of the accident, "and yes he'll be all right. He crashes it at least once a day, just to keep me on my toes. Don't feel obliged to follow – he'll just be a pig to you. You'll want to thump him and I'll feel embarrassed."

"Well, with an offer like that! How could I refuse?" he answered, striding to keep up with her. She seemed relaxed – if a little down-trodden – but he thought he'd better tag along, just in case this was the one time the crash-test dummy had taken his antics a step too far.

The younger children trailed behind them and he felt a tiny hand creep into one of his. The little boy. Scotty. The kid looked up at him, the same glowing, healthy looks as the rest of them. They all looked like adverts for Scandinavian log cabins, with their shining blonde hair and big blue eyes. Thoroughly disconcerting.

"Don't worry," said Lily – or maybe Daisy – as they passed. "Patrick's just a bit of a mollusc," said the other one, completing the sentence.

The mollusc in question was sprawled on the path, one of his legs trapped beneath what looked like an old Kawasaki. He wasn't wearing a helmet and his hair – predictably blonde, but a lot dirtier than the others' – was splayed across a face that was scratched raw with gravel burn. It had to hurt and would be a swine to clean with all those tiny scrapes pockmarked with even tinier stones.

Pippa paused, her lips twisting into a grimace, then walked over without a word. She leaned down, picked up the bike and threw it to one side. It bounced, the spokes whirring in the wind. Wow, thought Ben, she was stronger than she looked. Or maybe, he realised, it was just that she'd had a lot of practice – nobody was reacting as though this was an unusual occurrence, not even the younger kids. In fact, Daisy and Lily had their arms crossed over their chests and were mimicking the exasperated expression their big sister was wearing. Lord help the local boys with those two when they were older!

"This," she said, kicking her younger brother in his good leg with her mud-coated wellie, "is Patrick. Patrick, this is Ben Retallick. He's staying in Honeysuckle for the week. If you could try and avoid hitting him with the death machine, blowing up his belongings or stealing his car, I'd really appreciate it. What do you say?"

The teenager gazed up at them all, looking from his stern big sister to a confused-looking Ben. His sullen face, seared red by his scrapes, broke into a huge grin.

"Wow, sis!" he said, brushing himself down and standing up. "Do you know who this is?"

"Yes, Patrick, I do," she replied, sighing. "It's Ben Retallick. The boy who threw me in the duck pond when I was seven."

"Nah," he replied, staring at Ben as if he was the only interesting thing he'd ever seen in his whole existence. "This is Ben Retallick – that posh lawyer who got sent down for beating the shit out of some loser who got off with it. You remember? Bad Boy Ben, they called him – it was all over the bloody newspapers! Put the bloke in hospital for weeks! You treat me like I'm dirt 'cause PC Plod in the village has a whinge about me, sis, but you've gone and invited a proper ex-con into the family home – what *will* people say?"

Chapter 3

Pippa couldn't sleep, for about a million and one reasons, not all of them involving caffeine. After he'd dropped his bombshell – thrilled that he'd got one over on her – Patrick had limped off to the village saying he was going butterfly-hunting. That was a lie, clearly, and not even a good one. He was going to the pub. Everyone knew he was under-age, but as his birthday was only a few weeks off, the eyes of the staff were well and truly turned. They didn't see the harm – mainly because they didn't have to deal with the fallout. She was lucky enough to have that plum job.

He still wasn't back and she knew there was a strong possibility he wouldn't be – that he'd spend the night crashed out on a pal's sofa, in the nearest hay barn, with one of the girls who seemed smitten by his small-town Steve McQueen routine, or even on the beach. At least he wasn't on his bike this time, she thought. They'd played out this particular drama a hundred times before, and she knew it called for deep breaths and calming thoughts. He was a big boy – too big for a spanking. Too big for a cuddle. Although she suspected he'd probably needed both on regular occasions over the last few years, and she hadn't been parent enough to provide either. Possibly because she was only a few years older than him herself – physically, at least.

She'd tossed and turned so many times in her bed, worrying about him, about what he was doing. About what she wasn't doing.

About how she could try and reach him. About how she'd quite like it if he just buggered off and lived somewhere else.

That last one was usually the final stop on the late-night train ride through her brain. She knew Patrick – she loved Patrick. She understood why he was the way he was – but it didn't make it any easier to deal with.

That's when she usually reached the point where she had to try and talk herself down, get some rest so she could deal with the challenges of the next day. With the needs of the kids still young enough for her to matter to them – the ones she could still save, if Patrick was determined to plough his own destructive path.

The calming thoughts, though, just weren't coming that night. They were being chased away by all the anxious thoughts instead. And the anxious thoughts were bigger, nastier and came equipped with badass stun guns.

She couldn't stop the anxiety flooding over her, dozens of tiny and not-so-tiny concerns drowning her in a crushing wave. Like the fact that the second instalment of the tax bill was due at the end of the next month. That the dishwasher in Primrose needed replacing. That their account at the vet's was bigger than the national debt of a small African republic. That Social Services were due their quarterly visit in a few weeks' time, and they'd all need to scrub up, shape up and pass muster. Four times a year she had to prove that she was a suitable person to be raising the kids. That Patrick's problems weren't dragging them all down; that Scotty's issues at school were just due to shyness; that Daisy and Lily were communicating properly with the outside world.

She'd been doing this for years now, since she'd managed to convince them to take a risk on her after the car crash that claimed their parents. She was eighteen at the time and expected to head off to Oxford to study history. One drunk driver changed all that and instead she found herself playing mother to the other four, including baby Scotty. It wasn't what she'd planned for her life – but she couldn't stand by and watch them all get split up and packed off into foster care, could she? Not that the thought hadn't crossed her mind – she was eighteen. Nowhere near old enough to become a mother, she knew. And maybe, she thought, when Patrick was playing up and her self-esteem was hiding somewhere round her ankles, they'd all have been better off if she'd thrown in the towel.

But. . .well. They'd survived so far and they'd carry on surviving.

She kicked the covers off her with her feet, lying in the dark and staring at the shadowed ceiling, criss-crossed with wooden beams. She glanced at the clock and didn't like what she saw. Tomorrow was going to be an absolute bastard.

Her brain was just too busy to let her body go to sleep. It was all twisting and turning in there, like a barrel of angry snakes. Patrick, the money, Social Services – and, if she was honest, the man in the cottage across the way. Ben Retallick. Duckpond-slinger, cow-wrangler and convicted criminal.

Patrick's revelation had shocked *her*, but not Ben – his face had fallen into a well-worn mask, almost as though he'd been expecting it. As though he'd played this scene out before. No replies, no response to her brother's mockery or to her perplexed look. He gave them all a polite smile as he backed off, traipsed down the hill and retreated into Honeysuckle. No explanations. No comment at all, in fact. He'd shut the door behind him and never emerged again, not even when the rain cleared up and the sun started to shimmer gold onto the blues and greens of the Atlantic. He looked mega-fit, active, the type who went fell-running or surfing or at least cliff-walking. But he stayed in, presumably Minding His Own Business.

Which was certainly more than *she'd* managed. As soon as the kids had been packed off to bed – a long, multi-tiered process that involved stories, games of I-Spy, the forcible brushing of teeth and the collection of discarded underwear from the bathroom floor – she'd settled down with too much coffee and hooked up to her patchy internet access. It was frustrating, constantly having to reconnect, but she was used to it. All part of the charm, she told her guests, while swearing silently as she waited for pages to load. All she really wanted to do was watch an hour of crap telly and pass out, but she needed to know more about Ben Retallick. About Patrick's comments and about the kind of man who was staying in a cottage just a few short steps away from her and her family in the main farmhouse.

The online newspapers were full of stories about him – so much so that she couldn't believe she'd missed it. He must have been on the TV, on front pages, on billboards. Huge news in the local press. All over the known universe, in fact, and still it had slipped her notice. That's what running a business and raising four kids did for you, she thought. You lost your grip on the world at large – all that mattered were the concerns of daily life, getting through every blocked toilet and piece of homework and dentist's visit and random call from the local police. Feeding five humans and a menagerie of animals. Cleaning a farmhouse and three cottages and a barnyard and washing clothes for the whole tribe. Ironing school uniforms and plaiting hair and mowing the lawn and watering the plants and dealing with bookings and bills. It was endless and left approximately zero minutes per day for watching the news or reading tabloids. Frankly, she'd probably have missed a zombie apocalypse until the undead trudged over the hill looking for the next human limb to chomp on.

Now, though, she knew it all. Or at least knew what had been reported. She knew that Ben Retallick, up until two years ago, had been a celebrated criminal prosecution barrister living and working in London. He'd come a long way from the days of hangover recovery on a Cornish hillside.

That had all changed when he accepted a case involving Darren McConnell, a man who was accused of swindling pensioners out of their life savings. One of them had been so overcome with guilt at losing his and his wife's nest egg that he'd committed suicide, leaving evidence for the police of McConnell's involvement.

Eight other elderly couples came forward with their version of events, claiming McConnell had done the same to them. Ben Retallick, though, had not managed to secure a conviction – the evidence was all circumstantial, leaving the jury with enough doubt that they were unable to convict him.

The rest of the story came out at another court case – Ben's own. He was charged with criminal assault after beating McConnell so badly he was left with three broken ribs, a broken jaw and concussion. Various versions of events were recalled, but the conclusion seemed to be that McConnell had gone to see the lawyer after the case and thanked him for "letting him off". During the course of the conversation, he gloated about the fact that he had been guilty all along. That he'd stolen the money, that they'd been "asking for it", that he had no remorse. That he didn't give two hoots about the "old codger" who died.

Retallick had snapped and taken a swing at him. A fight ensued, with McConnell coming off much the worse – unsurprising as he was a weasel of man who ended up hospitalised. Ben had been sentenced to a year in jail and disbarred, despite a media campaign that portrayed him as a hero. The press came down mainly on his side, stressing the way the legal system had let the victims down, and that Ben Retallick had finally cracked under the pressure.

He'd never given an interview, never gone on the record outside the court case, never spoken publically about the mess his life was in, even after his release. In fact, he became something of a hermit, with near-legendary status – people snapped pictures of him on their mobiles and posted them on websites, reported sightings of him, wrote messages of support to newspapers. Someone had even set up a fake Twitter account in his name with photoshopped pictures of Big Bad Ben taking down historic villains with a handy right hook.

McConnell might have been the victim – and there were plenty of pictures of him with his taped-up ribs, matching black eyes and head bandage – but Ben came out as the one people sympathised with. Ben Retallick was a criminal – but he was one the nation very much approved of. Despite his silence, newspapers and columnists were still debating the rights and wrongs of the whole fiasco. A convicted criminal or a national hero, depending on your point of view.

Exactly which Ben Retallick was here, with her family, Pippa wondered? Hiding out in Honeysuckle Cottage. Moments away. Probably asleep, although the light was still burning in his bedroom window. What should she do about it? He'd seemed a nice man, a calm man. A thinker, not a fighter. He'd even helped with the recalcitrant cow. Yet the photos didn't lie – he'd come close to killing McConnell, and no matter how much he might have deserved it, that kind of violence was frightening.

As she often did when she was troubled, Pippa turned to her parents for answers. She twisted around in bed, looked at the framed photo of them on the cabinet. A rare shot of all of them together, Scotty a babe in arms, Patrick lurking in the background, already looking sullen and angry with the world – as though he knew the world was going to punch him in the face even before it actually did.

Marissa and Stuart Harte had been kind people. They never judged and they'd raised their kids to do the same. They were always encouraged to think freely, to use their own instincts. To trust their own feelings. Even if that ended up getting them dunked in a duck pond.

And that, she thought, climbing out of the tangled sheets and pulling on a pair of old tracksuit trousers and a vest top, was exactly what she had to do now. She needed to follow their lead and trust her instincts. Use her own judgement – not that of the tabloid press.

She checked in on the kids as she tiptoed down the hallway, avoiding the patches of old wooden floorboard that creaked – they needed replacing, which was coming in at about number ninety-eight on her to-do list. Daisy and Lily were top-to-tail in one bed, as usual, even though they each had their own, and Scotty was crumpled up in his traditional tiny ball of warm flesh. His hair was too long, she thought, seeing it stuck to his forehead in blonde clumps. She lingered an extra moment, the sweetness of the sight filling her heart and chasing away at least some of the strain of the day. Bless him. He was the anti-Patrick – for now at least. With her parenting skills, though, he could be a criminal mastermind by the time he was ten.

Satisfied they were all firmly in the land of nod, she crept downstairs and slipped out of the side door, crossing the cobbles to Honeysuckle, realising it was too chilly for flip-flops. She paused and looked up at the cottage. The light was still on. She wouldn't be waking him. And even if she was… well, it had to be done, and it pretty much had to be done now.

She knocked lightly as her hair flew around her face in the wind. Not quite gale force, but the waves would be crashing into the cove. She could hear them rolling in already. She hoped Patrick had found somewhere more civilised to bunk for the night, then switched that train of thought off – there was nothing she could do about Patrick. Not right now, probably not ever.

Ben opened the door, interior light flooding around him as he looked down at her. She took a gulp and hoped it wasn't audible. He was wearing only a battered pair of faded Levis and his hair was damp from the shower he'd obviously just taken. Tiny droplets of water had scattered over broad shoulders and the moonlight played over the smooth, dark skin of his bare chest, even the small movement of holding the door open showing her the ripple of muscle in his arms. A fine line of silky black hair trailed down into the waistband of his jeans, and she tried not to stare at it. She was here for answers, not to lech, she reminded herself.

"Can I come in?" she asked simply, and he moved back, inviting her into the cottage that technically she owned. She sat down on one of the squashy armchairs and noted the open laptop with a screen full of text, a glass of rich amber liquid next to it. At least she hadn't woken him. Maybe he had badass stun gun-wielding worries in his brain as well.

"Whisky and work," he said, grabbing a black t-shirt and pulling it on. "The two essentials of my life. Want one?"

He held up the bottle – the label looked Scottish and expensive – and she shook her head. She rarely ever drank, and this didn't seem like a good time to start.

"What is work now...after, you know…?" she asked.

He settled down opposite her, looking no less attractive for being clothed, but certainly less distracting.

"Why? Are you worried I won't be able to pay my bill?"

"That's not what I meant at all...and I didn't mean to pry, but I'm sure you can imagine I have some questions."

"Yeah. I can. To answer one of them, I'm writing a book. My second – the first is due out later this year. And no, it's not about me and what happened – although there were plenty of offers to do just that. It's a legal thriller. I've wanted to do it for years, but never had the time. Now, I have nothing but time, and a three-book publishing deal to keep me occupied. Next?"

She took a breath, wondered if she should have accepted that whisky after all. Time to belly-flop into the deep end – small talk would get them nowhere.

"I didn't know anything about it," she said. "Honestly, I didn't. To me, you were just the boy from the duck pond. The last few years have been. . .well, busy. I've not exactly been keeping up with current events, and I had no idea what Patrick was talking about earlier. But thanks to the magic of the internet, now I do. Or at least one version of it."

He was silent, waiting for more. Ben had been expecting this all day, from the minute her oik of a brother had recognised him – expecting to get his marching orders, or to be asked for his autograph. He'd known both to happen. When she didn't continue, he asked, "Okay. So now you know. Why are you here? Have you come to ask me to leave?"

"No," she replied simply. "I said I know one version of it. Now, I want to know yours."

He smiled at her, but to Pippa it looked like a bitter, twisted thing, full of frustration and controlled fury. His eyes were downcast, his hair falling across his forehead. Beneath the thin jersey of his shirt, she could see packed muscle bunching and releasing in tension as he breathed hard and fast. His large hands were clenched into fists, and he was biting down on his lower lip, as though he was trying to keep angry words inside. No, McConnell wouldn't have stood a chance. And neither would she, if he went all Hulk on her right now.

"Why do you want to know?" he finally said, reaching out and snapping the lid of the laptop shut with a dull thud. "And why should I tell you? I've kept quiet all this time. The only person I tried to talk to about it...well, she made her feelings quite clear. She left me as soon as I was found guilty. She didn't want to know the truth and after that I decided there was nobody else important enough to tell. Certainly not reporters or complete strangers, even one I threw in a duck pond once upon a time. Why should I tell you?"

Pippa leaned towards him, which was harder than it looked in the squashy chair. She stared him in the eye, wanting him to know that she wasn't going to give up.

"I want to know because you're living here, with us," she said. "With my family. With people I love, people it's my job to protect. That's the only reason. Believe me, I've no interest in the dirty details, or sharing anything with the rest of the world. As I think we've already established, I'm not exactly plugged into the rest of the world. I just need to know that I can trust you. My instinct says I can, but I need to hear it from you before I can relax and allow you to remain here with us.

"I'm sorry you were hurt, but that was nothing to do with me, and that's not my burden to carry. My responsibility to the kids is. So I need you to tell me why you did it. That simple."

He looked up, surprised at her choice of words. Simple? Nothing about it was simple, he thought. She sat there, swamped in that stupidly chintzy chair, dressed like a homeless teenager, hair falling over her shoulders and back like a yellow waterfall. One flip-flop dangling half off her foot. Her eyes were direct and clear, her expression calm and still. She was waiting for him to reassure her, to tell her his version of events. Wanting him to back up her instincts, but wary. A tigress looking out for her cubs.

Not simple at all – but at least, he supposed, she was giving him a chance. She hadn't made up her mind, not like Johanna and her family. And, he realised, he believed her when she said she wasn't looking for the dirty details. She wasn't prying – she was safeguarding her territory. Could he blame her for that? Wasn't that what any decent mother would do? It was certainly a better motivation than pure nosiness.

He raked his hands through his hair, reminded himself that he needed to get it cut. Without the need to head into an office every day, these things had a tendency to slip. He sipped the whisky, grimaced as it burned down his throat.

Finally, he looked up. Met the cornflower-blue gaze, glanced at the determined tilt of her head, the stubborn set of her full lips. A child, really. That's all she was – and yet she was having the strangest effect on him, making him feel calm and settled at the same time she made him feel hyper-aware of her physical presence. The way his body was responding to it. It was hard to think straight and unlikely to get any easier the longer he let this moment linger.

"Some of the stories were right," he said, staring off through the window into the still darkness of the courtyard. He hadn't told this story before – not properly – and he needed a small sense of distance to allow him to get the words out.

"It was partly the pressure. I'd been prosecuting for while by then, and I did the best I could. But you always feel the dice are loaded against you. The paperwork, the bureaucracy, the loopholes. McConnell got to me and I shouldn't have allowed him to. Maybe a year earlier, he wouldn't have done, who knows? But that case...he was so clearly *guilty*. He'd destroyed the lives of so many people, older people who'd worked hard all their lives. People like my granddad, who lost his farm to the banks when he couldn't make farming work any more. Maybe that's why it touched a nerve, I don't know."

He paused, poured himself another drink. God knew he needed it. Pippa remained still and quiet, her legs tucked beneath her as she listened. The neon-orange flip-flops had dropped to the floor, lying there criss-crossed.

"I always knew it would be hard to make the case," he continued. "The evidence was flimsy, when it came down to it. He'd been clever, covered his tracks well. I knew, his lawyer knew, the jury knew that he'd done it. But the way our system works, we couldn't make it stick. It was depressing and even before I'd been thinking of quitting. I couldn't take it much more and watching him walk was the final straw. I thought it was – at least. Until that night, when he found me in my office. He was drunk, been out celebrating his freedom.

"He came to gloat, to push, to confess. Rub my nose in it. He actually laughed about the man who killed himself, said it was survival of the fittest, that he'd done his wife a favour, because at least she had the insurance money now. There was no remorse – he didn't even see them as people. Just old, weak victims.

"What can I say? I lost my temper. I hit him. He hit me back. We fought. You know what happened next. I shouldn't have done it – I know that. I've always regretted it, not just because of what happened to me, but because it was wrong. Stooping to that level, it made me as bad as the people I'd been trying to put away. The papers can talk as much as they want about me being on the side of the angels, but I was wrong. I'd never done anything like that before and I never will again. Afterwards, when I looked down at him crumpled on the floor of my office, when I called the ambulance and saw my knuckles were scraped and scarred and my hands were covered in his blood, I was sickened. Sickened by what I'd done. What I'd allowed myself to become. And I've regretted it every single day since."

He stopped, looked at her, his eyes shining with the pain of the memory, his voice rough, tense, his breath coming in fierce bursts, as though he'd worn himself out forcing the words she'd asked him to share.

"Is that what you wanted to know?" he asked, as she studied him intently, still silent. "Because I can tell you more...I can tell you how many times I hit him, how it felt when my fist slammed into his jaw; how hard it was to control myself and stop...or do you want to know what prison was like? How I've walked outside every single day since I got out, to try and clean myself of the memory? Do you want to know what my fiancée said about it on the day she left me there? Is that what you want to know?"

"No," Pippa replied quietly, getting to her feet and tugging her top down, tucking stray hair behind her ears. She slipped her feet back into the flip-flops and looked up to face him. "That's enough. That's all I need. Thank you for explaining. I know it was hard for you, but I needed to hear it."

He stood, looked at her, feeling the familiar anguish well up inside him. Waiting for the "but". It had been a long time since he'd discussed this with anyone and he felt sick to his stomach even thinking about it. The whisky ran warm through him and he realised – completely inappropriately – that it had also been a long time since he'd been with a woman. Almost two years since he'd felt the touch of soft skin, the drape of long hair in his hands, since his fingers had skimmed delicate curves.

He closed that thought down and waited for the verdict, hovering next to her as she prepared to leave. With Johanna, he had expected forgiveness. The reassurance that she loved him and they would get through this together. The touch of her fingers twined in his, the feel of her lips promising she'd be there for him. That she understood, and that she'd wait for him – that they'd still build a life together.

He'd been wrong to expect any of that, and the memory of the cold sheen in her eyes was something he would always carry with him. It had been a stark lesson in what women were capable of: a ruthlessness he'd never seen before. She'd shut him out, closed him down, thrown him out with the trash and moved on to better things. The papers could call him a hero as much as they liked – but headlines didn't keep you warm at night. They didn't love you, give you hope or belief in the future. He hadn't had any of those things for a very long time – thanks to his own actions and Johanna's response.

And now here he was again, having poured out his heart, waiting for a woman's verdict – and with almost as much tension as he'd felt in court. This was the part, he knew, where Pippa Harte told him to pack his bags and leave, and did it all with a sweet smile.

Off you go, Mr Retallick! Don't let the barn door hit you on the arse on the way out...He was braced, he was ready. In fact he hadn't even unpacked at all, just in case – just plugged in the laptop to charge, showered and changed clothes, and left everything else in his bags. He had his polite smile ready for when she told him to sling his hook – or at least phoned him a cab, because he'd drank far too much whisky to be driving.

Instead, she reached out. Took one of his hands and gently squeezed it, as he'd seen her do with Scotty that afternoon. He felt the shock of the unexpected contact like a delicious slap: her slender fingers in his, all that glorious hair only inches away. The tempting shape of her body beneath her shabby old clothes.

"That's enough," she said. "The rest is private. I know what I need to know. I'm so sorry that happened to you, all of it. And we'd be glad to welcome you at Harte Farm for as long as you need to stay. Just try and keep a low profile – the last thing I need is the villagers deciding to throw you a street party or storming the castle with pitchforks. But...stay. Enjoy the place, for as long as you're here."

He was stunned. Silent. Flooded with emotion at her gentle acceptance, the way she looked up at him, her eyes liquid. Her hand, warm, soft, still in his. Sweet Jesus – this slip of a girl, this virtual stranger, had given him more comfort and consolation in that one short speech than he'd received in the last eighteen months. It warmed him even more than the whisky.

"Thank you," he murmured, pulling her gently towards him, needing to feel her against him. To share the way he felt, even for a second. She came, taking tiny steps, and laid her head against his chest. He could feel her breath, hot and fast against him; could smell the lavender of her shampoo, the slight tremble in her arms as they slid around his waist, briefly stroking his lower back before she slipped back out of reach.

"Now I'd better get to bed," she murmured. "Before I start letting out war cries and jumping on your head."

He watched her go – face flushed, breasts rising and falling, eyes blinking too rapidly – and knew that she'd felt it too. That moment. That magical moment between a man and a woman, where you feel the thrill of potential, the primal joy of heat calling out to heat.

Scarier than a war cry any day, he thought, as the door slammed shut behind her and she disappeared back out into the darkness.

Chapter 4

By the time the roosters started calling, Pippa had already been awake for an hour. Her days always started early, but this, she thought, glugging coffee, was ridiculous. Up and about by 5am, ready to get the feeds done and crack on with some paperwork.

She grimaced as she drank the last cooling dregs, tried to convince herself it was a good head start to the day. Except it didn't feel like that. She normally valued these quiet hours before the rest of the family got up, the time on her own to think, to plan. To eat chocolate digestives and occasionally have a little cry.

But today was different. Today, she didn't feel alone – because her head was full of Ben Retallick. Full of his story, his sadness, the pain in his chocolate-brown eyes. Full of the feel of him as they'd embraced, the way it felt to run her fingers over the packed muscle of his back, the way her heart sped up the minute he touched her. It was all...weird.

She wasn't a blushing virgin by any means, but her sexual experience was limited to one boyfriend several years ago. And when he'd touched her, it certainly hadn't felt anything like the fireworks that had popped in psychedelic glory when Ben held her the night before.

Growing up on a farm, you got your sex education the natural way – but at no time in her life had she experienced anything like the flood of sensation she'd felt in Ben's arms.

All he'd done was hold her, wrap her in his arms as she leaned into him. It was comfort, it was innocent. It was one human being in need recognising another. And yet...she'd left Honeysuckle a mess. Knowing that it would have been so easy to raise her head to his, to invite his lips. To invite his touch. To invite absolute chaos into a life that was already pretty ragged around the edges. If he'd wanted more – if he'd wanted to throw her on the floor and ravish her – she wouldn't have been able to stop him. Wouldn't have even wanted to. Luckily, she thought, he'd been a gentleman. Even though part of her was wishing he hadn't been.

She needed to get a grip. She didn't have the time for a relationship, no matter how much her body told her it wanted one. She didn't even have time for a mindless quickie on the shag pile of Honeysuckle, for goodness sake. That could all come later, when the kids were older. When life was more settled. She'd switched off those thoughts years ago, set it all aside. It hadn't been easy – but there was so much else to do.

She wasn't a saint, she had her moments of desperation. Of self-pity. Of wishing she had someone else's life. For one small period she'd hoarded travel brochures in her bedroom, giving in to fantasies about jacking it all in – letting Social Services take the kids and backpacking around Asia to find herself. Or lose herself, whichever came first. But that's all they were: fantasies. Even they left her with the guilt hangover from hell, when Lily and Daisy had found the glossy magazines and asked if they were going away on holiday.

So she compartmentalised, as the books say. Learned to set aside her own needs and focus on everyone else's so hard she almost forgot she had any. It had seemed the only way to cope.

Until now, until last night, it had been working. Last night she seemed to have regressed to being a love-struck teenager, wondering how it would feel to slip her hands beneath that t-shirt;

to have him bury his hands in her hair. How it would feel to put her skin next to his and let all that heat take its course.

She'd be doodling his name on a pencil case inside a loveheart next, she thought, shaking her head in an effort to clear it. This was real life, not a romance novel: and real life was busy. Hard. Challenging in every single way. She didn't have time for mooning around, or for imagining Ben naked, or even for drinking coffee and staring out of the window down to the bay.

Her thoughts were interrupted by the phone ringing and she felt a swoosh of panic flow through her. Phone calls late at night or this early in the morning never meant anything good. It's not as if it was going to be the man from the Premium Bonds telling her she was a millionaire, or even a utility company trying to persuade her to change supplier. Not at this time of day.

She lifted the receiver, muttered a cautious hello.

"Sis? Is that you?" said Patrick, his voice low and whispering.

Patrick. Of course. She'd glimpsed into his room when she'd woken up and seen that he wasn't there. At least she thought he wasn't. It was hard to tell for sure under all the mess. She'd expected him to roll up in a few hours, hung over and smelly, as usual. Except he was calling her – and sounding scared.

"Yes, of course it's me. Who else would it be?" she replied, trying to hold down her temper. After all, for once her agitated mental state wasn't Patrick's fault – it wasn't down to him that she'd been tossing and turning all night. "What's wrong?"

"I don't know what to do, sis," he replied, voice urgent and sounding way younger than usual. "Me and Robbie got into a bit of trouble last night. We didn't mean anything by it, honest, but we went a bit too far. It was after the pub. Old man Jensen had been in there, winding us up, telling us all those stupid stories about what he was doing at our age – all that crap about the war. So later, after we'd had a skinful, we went round to his house. We only meant to scare him, maybe throw a few bricks at the window, whatever. But...well, we got carried away. Made a real mess of the garden. Broke the windscreen of that ancient Volvo he drives round in. And, well, the thing is, I think he saw us."

She couldn't tell which he was most upset about – that he'd done this awful thing, or that he'd been spotted. If it was the latter, she didn't know what she could do for him. Please God, she thought, closing her eyes and clenching back the tears that were stinging at her tired eyes, let him actually regret it. She so didn't need this right now – not with the review coming up. Not with her mind full of Ben. Not ever.

She felt like hanging up. Giving up. Entirely possibly shooting up.

"Okay," she said, keeping her voice calm despite her inner turmoil. If she screamed at him, he'd bolt. He'd do one of his disappearing acts and leave her fretting for days on end. "Where are you now?"

"In that phone box by the Surf Shack. Mine's out of charge. Robbie's still crashed in the back of his car. What should I do, sis?"

She wanted to yell at him, "Grow up!" but she didn't. Instead she took a deep breath and told him to stay where he was. That she'd come and get him.

Then she put the phone down and wondered how exactly she was going to manage that. How she could leave the kids alone, feed the animals and rescue her brother all at the same time. Yet another impossible day stretched ahead of her.

She looked up at the kitchen clock. Almost six. The kids would be awake soon. Scotty would be climbing into her bed looking for a cuddle and the twins would be ready to rampage their way through another day. The guests in Foxglove were settled, so no worries there. And the elderly couple in Primrose had gone to Penzance for the night. Which only left...Ben.

Could she ask him for help? Should she? It seemed as though she had no alternative. Yet again, Patrick had her boxed into a corner.

Pippa got up, rinsed out her coffee mug and looked across the courtyard to Honeysuckle. The curtains were open in the living room. Looked like Mr Retallick was an early riser as well – that or he'd had problems sleeping too.

She made her decision and walked across the cobbles. Before she'd even had chance to knock, the door opened. At least, she thought, he was dressed this time. Although the damage was already done – her brain had logged every inch of his bare torso last night and her imagination was keeping it on file for future reference. She could replay it with a glass of wine later.

"Hi," he said. "You're up early...is everything okay? You look terrible."

"I bet you say that to all the girls," she replied, suddenly conscious of her unbrushed hair, the fact that her denims had holes in the knees, that she hadn't worn make-up for what felt like years. Not that any of it mattered, she told herself. Those were things other girls worried about. She had more pressing concerns.

"I'm really sorry to ask," she said, "but I wondered if you could do me a favour?"

An hour later, she pulled up in the driveway, the wheels of the battered Land Rover spitting gravel the same way she felt like spitting swear words. Holding it all in, she unlatched the door of the farmhouse, Patrick following silently behind her. She was desperate to see how the kids were, hoping against hope that they'd all stayed in bed for a lie-in.

Instead, they seemed to have got up early and decided to start a bakery business.

The twins were at the kitchen table mixing currants into a big bowl of dough. Scotty was standing on a chair by the counter using his tiny fists to knead another bowl of slop. And Ben – he was standing right next to him, making sure he didn't slip.

"Pippa!" said Lily and Daisy in unison. "We're making scones for breakfast!"

"I see that," replied Pippa, "weren't cornflakes good enough today?"

"We've built up quite an appetite," said Ben, flicking on the kettle and preparing a mug of coffee for her. "We've done the morning feed and mucked out Harry Potter. That was fun. I'd forgotten quite how...productive pigs could be. A magic wand would have been quite helpful. So...now we're preparing a feast. I hope that's okay? I promise we all washed our hands very thoroughly."

He handed her the coffee and she grabbed it gratefully, using the hot china to warm her shaking hands. It was still early, still chilly and her life was still a mess.

Yes, she wanted to say, of course that's okay. But...she felt weird. It was odd coming in here, back into the family kitchen and seeing him in it. Seeing the kids so happy and occupied. Seeing Scotty without him running straight to her for a hug. Seeing Ben leaning against the counter, hair all messed up and his face smudged with flour. Looking right at home.

For years, it had only been them. The occasional visitor from the village, but mainly just them. Now she felt like her territory was being... invaded, somehow. She felt like she should ask him to leave: they were fine before he arrived and they'd be fine after he left. She could make her own scones, even if they did always burn around the edges. It wasn't rational – but it was definitely there, like an eyelash stuck under her lid.

She pulled herself together, reminded herself that Ben had been invited. That he'd done her a favour. A big one. And that she should be happy to have had some of her chores done. The man had shovelled pig poo for her, for goodness' sake! She smiled and nodded, watched as he lifted Scotty carefully down from his perch and sat him at the table. Everything felt way too calm – or maybe it was only chaos when she was around. Ben certainly seemed to have everything under control. She could tell from the white powdery smears around Scotty's mouth that he'd even brushed his teeth.

As she sipped the hot coffee, her spider senses tingled, and she turned around in time to see Patrick trying to slink off into the background. She fixed him with a stern look and placed one firm hand on his chest.

"Front room," she said. "Now."

He pulled a face, but did as he was told – which was damn-near miraculous. She followed him and realised that Ben was right behind her. She looked up at his concerned face, wondering exactly how rude it would be shut him out now. To tell him politely that his services were no longer required, and that he should bugger off back to Honeysuckle. There was still an hour before they had to leave for school – plenty of time for her to do everything herself. Which felt, somehow, safer.

"I might be able to help," he said simply, as though sensing her hesitation. She nodded in return. Maybe he could. It's not like he was inexperienced in the ways of troubled youth or criminal damage. And she knew, deep down, that she was reacting like this out of stubbornness – she'd done everything on her own for so long, she'd forgotten how to accept help at all. Which, she knew, was downright stupid.

Patrick slumped sullenly into one of the armchairs, refusing to make eye contact with either of them. Her heart broke to look at him: his beautiful hair dirty and long, his face streaked with scratches from his latest crash. Reeking of beer, wearing the same clothes he'd had on for days. He hadn't always been like this. Sure, he'd been a sulky kid – but after their parents died, something seemed to die inside him as well, rotting away until he was incapable of recapturing any joy that didn't come out of a bottle. He'd never really talked about it and had always fought her pathetic attempts at authority – which was completely understandable as

she was only a teenager herself at the time. She didn't even respect her own authority.

Now, a few years wiser and what felt like a hundred years older, she had the "don't give me any crap" glare down to perfection. After a few prompts, he told his story – with a scattering of "it wasn't my faults" and "it got a bit out of hands" thrown in. He didn't even look like he believed them himself, and she certainly didn't. Robbie was trouble, always had been – but Patrick didn't need his help to find it. He'd vandalised an innocent man's property for petty kicks, and now seemed to be trying to convince himself he was blameless. She clung to that thought – that the act was as much for his own conscience as hers. At least that would mean he had one.

At the end of it, she looked at him, then looked at Ben, who'd stayed quiet apart from a few salient questions.

"What do you think we should do, Ben?" she asked. She had her own opinions on that, but as one of the top legal minds in the country was sitting in her front room, she might as well make use of him.

"I think," he said slowly, "that we need to pay a visit to Mr Jensen."

Chapter 5

"I knew your grandfather," said Mr Jensen, after they'd all settled in for cups of tea.

They'd found him sweeping glass out of his driveway, surrounded by black plastic bin bags as he tried to sort out some of the chaos Patrick and Robbie had caused in his garden. He'd taken one look at them – Pippa doing her best to smile, Ben politely introducing himself and Patrick mumbling apologies – and invited them in. His wife had died years earlier, but despite his advanced age he kept his house as neat as a pin.

"Really?" said Ben. "He passed away a few years ago."

"I know that," replied Mr Jensen. "It was the banks that did for him. He was never the same after he lost the farm. Only in his late eighties as well – a waste of a man."

Pippa held back a smile, amused despite the circumstances – maybe when she reached that age, she'd think of late eighties as being young as well. Although the way Patrick was going, she'd never make it that far. She'd pop her clogs from sheer shock well before she got her bus pass.

She also wondered why she hadn't heard more about Ben's grandfather dying. The tone of Mr Jensen's voice and the slight clenching of Ben's fists told her there was more to that story than either of them was mentioning. This part of Cornwall was a village;

if there'd been anything unusual, she would have heard...except, well. If it had happened near the time of the deaths of her parents, there'd only been one story that interested her. Her own.

"Got into a bit of trouble yourself a bit back, didn't you?" Mr Jensen continued, in that shamelessly blunt way the very old often have, peering at Ben over the edge of his teacup. His eyes were narrowed, hidden in the folds of so many wrinkles you could barely see them. It was a good face, a face that had spent a lot of time outside, crinkled up against the wind.

"I did, Mr Jensen – but I've served my time. Paid my debt to society, as they say. Which is what we're hoping you'll let Patrick do."

The old man made a "harrumphing" noise, seeming to ponder it.

"I was about to call the police when you lot turned up. I saw them last night, those two, thinking they're all clever like. Clever as my septic tank. Suppose you think I'm just an old fuddy duddy with nothing worth saying, don't you? Do you think I've reached the age where I should just shrivel up and die, son, clear a bit of space at the bar?" he said, fixing Patrick with a stare that made him squirm.

"No! And I'm really sorry...I'll fix all the mess, Mr Jensen. Me and Robbie, we'll sort it out, I promise. We'd had too much to drink, that's all. I can't even remember most of it!"

"Aye. I saw that. Saw you staggering around out there, falling over my garden gnomes as you ran away. And I've been in that position myself before now, lad. I wasn't born this old, you know. I raised a bit of hell myself when I was your age – before I grew up and started raising my own family instead. That'll calm a man down. Or a woman."

He stared at them both, and Pippa knew he'd be thinking about their parents. Everyone knew what had happened to them. Everyone knew what she was trying to do. And everyone knew that Patrick was heading for a bad place. It wasn't uncommon in rural villages for the younger lads to play wild, but he was pushing it too far.

"Please, Mr Jensen," she added. "Let him make up for it. He'll pay for the damage to the car as well. I'll make sure he does. Just don't call the police – give him another chance."

"What do you reckon, son?" he asked Ben. "And how did you get mixed up in all this in the first place?"

"I just got lucky, I suppose, Mr Jensen. And I reckon Patrick deserves the chance to make this up to you. Like you said, you've been there yourself. Give him the opportunity to show you what he's made of. You know that if the police get involved, it'll be bad for him, and for Pippa and the children. Is that something you really want to live with?"

Pippa felt her face pale; Ben had said what she was thinking, but what she hadn't wanted to say. It was the truth, but it felt too much like emotional blackmail. She'd never played the pity card and didn't feel entirely comfortable with Ben doing it on her behalf. Unless it worked – then she'd just have to find a way to be comfortable with it.

"I reckon not," Mr Jensen said after a tense moment passed. "Not yet, anyway. You're doing a grand job, Pippa, and a hard job. This layabout brother of yours isn't helping, is he, love? Old enough to know better, he is, and instead he's got you all upset like this...he should be bloody well ashamed of himself."

"I am, honest," muttered Patrick, staring at his boots as intensely as Mr Jensen was staring at him.

"All right," he finally said. "It's a deal – but I want this place cleaned up quick smart, and I want a bit of help around the house. The garden. I'm almost ninety now. I could do with a pair of young hands to do the weeding. Twice a week should do to start with. I can tell them stories about my war days while they're at it."

He gave her a sly wink as he said it. Wily old coot.

Pippa saw Patrick bridle, about to complain, and gave him a "shut your mouth right now" look. It was a good deal and they took it, leaving Mr Jensen with the promise that Patrick would be back that afternoon – with his partner in crime.

"I'm off, sis," said Patrick as they stood outside in the pale sunshine. Honey bees hummed around the foxgloves and skylarks were singing over the distant fields. It would have been beautiful, if it hadn't been marred by her ASBO brother.

"Off where?" she asked harshly, arms crossed over her chest, feeling about a hundred and two.

"Don't worry – not the pub. It's not even open yet. I'm off to get some rubble sacks and to find Robbie. And...well, thanks. Both of you. I'll try not to cock up again too soon."

For a minute she thought he was going to hug her, but that would have been a detente too far. Instead, he shrugged and strode off down the hill towards the village. Where, indeed, the pub was still closed for another half an hour. She stared after him, noticing how big he'd got. He was turning into a man, physically at least. Eventually he'd leave home, and part of her – part of her she wasn't proud of – was looking forward to it.

"Come on," said Ben, putting his arm around her shoulder. "I'm taking you out for lunch."

"No!" she said, pulling away. "I have to pick the kids up from school!"

"Yes," he replied, looking at his watch, "in about four hours. I don't know about you, but I need a pint."

"He wasn't always like this," said Pippa, sipping her orange juice in the beer garden of The Stag. She'd deliberately directed him to a touristy pub well out of the village, free of locals, not wanting to attract any more attention. Not that she expected the paparazzi to leap out of the Cornish hedgerows, but...better safe than sorry. And she certainly didn't want to run the risk of finding Patrick in the village boozer, toasting her stupidity and laughing about his close scrape. She really hoped that wasn't what he was doing, but who knew?

"No?" queried Ben, who was casting his mind back all those years and recalling a younger Patrick, already taciturn and sneaky.

"No. He wasn't the life and soul of the party, but he was okay. A good kid. We fought like cat and dog even then, but it was all... normal. It was after they died. Our parents. He was only fourteen, and he didn't know how to cope. It's not his fault."

"I'm pretty sure," replied Ben, "that none of you knew how to cope, Pippa. Scotty must have been a baby. You were only a kid yourself. And the more you keep telling yourself it's not his fault, the more he'll keep taking advantage of you."

Pippa felt anger whip up inside her – what did he know? What did he know about Patrick, and her, and everything they'd gone through? A dozen retorts sprung to mind – all of them variations on "that's none of your business" – but she bit them back. After all, she'd just made it his business by dragging him into Patrick's latest escapade. And maybe...maybe he was right. She just didn't know any more. She'd never had anybody to talk to about it before. She'd become an island and a tsunami was rushing in towards the shore.

"But what about you?" he asked. "Did you always used to be like this? What were you like before the accident? And please don't tell me you never evolved from dressing up as Rambo and jumping on unsuspecting visitors' heads..."

"What do you mean, like this?" she asked, gesturing at her tattered jeans and wild hair. "I've always been this well groomed! I know I look like a mess – in fact I am a mess – but there never seems to be the time for anything more than brushing my teeth and falling into bed."

"That's not what I meant, no," he said, reaching out to place a hand over hers on the gnarled wooden tabletop. "And you look just fine. Better than fine. What I meant was, what were you going to do? If everything had gone to plan?"

"Ah. Gone to plan," she said, distracted by the feel of his skin on hers. Even the mildest of touches sent a flush into her cheeks, which she desperately tried to ignore. It was embarrassing apart from anything else.

"Well, I suppose I would have gone off to Oxford, where I had a place to study history. After that, who knows? Maybe teaching? Maybe archaeology? I always quite liked the thought of scrabbling around in the mud for a living...which is kind of what I do now, but without the priceless artefacts. Unless there's a secret Roman hoard lying underneath Bottom Paddock. That would be nice. It was that summer they died – the one between doing my A levels and going to uni. There wasn't any family, apart from some cousins in Canada, so I didn't have much of an alternative. Either I stayed or the kids went off into foster care. And really, can you imagine anyone wanting to take Patrick on without having to?"

She was joking, trying to make light of it, he knew. But he couldn't imagine how hard it must have been – for a girl who was obviously so bright, with her whole future ahead of her, to face that kind of decision. He'd spent years in court listening to sob stories about youths from broken homes, who used dysfunctional parents as an excuse for stealing cars and ram-raiding supermarkets. Yet she'd shown the strength of will to stay, to care for the tribe, to try and make it work. No wonder she didn't have time to get her nails done.

He found himself twining his fingers closer into hers, not wanting to break the connection. Her nails might be short and uncared for, but they were attached to her hands, her arms, her body. That crazy hair and the curves he could see outlined beneath her top. The whole package. He looked at her and wanted her – the way he'd never expected to want a woman again. He needed his head examining and briefly considered banging it against the wooden tabletop to try and knock some sense back into it.

"You did the right thing," he said. "But not the easy thing. Maybe you should give yourself a break? Even professional parents get things wrong sometimes. And the twins and Scotty seem like delightful kids. Patrick? Well, he's almost a grown man. There's only so much you can do."

Pippa looked into his eyes, feeling herself suddenly short of breath. They were surrounded by people and yet she felt as though they were alone. The only two survivors in the war of life. What would it be like, she wondered, to just lean forward and kiss him? He'd probably fall backwards off the bench and clonk his head on the next table.

"You're very wise, Mr Retallick," she said, "for one so young."

"Ha! I'm a lot older than you, Miss Harte, thanks for reminding me. And I'm not wise – look at the mess I made of my own life. A criminal record, no career, no wife, no family. I don't think I'd win any prizes, do you?"

"I don't know," she answered, a wicked grin creasing her face, "depends what kind of competition you were entering. There's a few farm shows around here where you can win rosettes for prize stud..."

"Are you flirting with me?" he asked, suddenly aware of an embarrassing reaction in his jeans. Down, boy, he told it. She's just flirting – not asking you out for kicks and giggles.

"Flirting...why, I think I just might be," she answered, a look of fake shock on her face. "It's been so long I barely recognised it. And I'm sorry if it makes you feel a bit sick, but it's your own fault. You're holding my hand and I did notice you were sniffing my hair earlier. That's asking for trouble, really, isn't it? I'm very out of practice, though, so I apologise for my lack of finesse. That's another thing I haven't had time for."

"Flirting?" he said, aware she was trying to lighten the tone. Avoid the big subjects – and who could blame her? Wasn't flirting a lot more fun than pondering death and disaster? Maybe she needed the distraction. Maybe he did too...

"Men in general. I haven't had a boyfriend since I was seventeen, and he wasn't up to much either. Although he did brew his own scrumpy, which was a definite plus point back then. In fact it probably explained why he was my boyfriend at all. What about you? You had a fiancée, you said? What happened? Why aren't you happily married and pumping out little Retallicks?"

"I would have been," he said, gently removing his hand from hers. "But she had different ideas. It appeared that life with a convict was not to Johanna's taste and she moved on."

"Just like that?" said Pippa, feeling her senses deflate now that his fingers were no longer entwined with hers.

"Just like that. We'd been engaged for over a year and the wedding was set for the October. But she, and her family, decided that I was no longer acceptable. No longer up to scratch. It wasn't about money – I had plenty saved up, and there was always the back-up plan of writing the book – it was about me. I didn't fit the profile any more."

"But that's crazy! You hadn't changed – you were the same person you always were, the same person she fell in love with in the first place!"

Ben laughed, but it was a sound devoid of humour. He was reminded again that despite her strength of character, Pippa Harte was still very young – and he needed to remember that. She was just a girl, no matter how much he enjoyed flirting with her. She'd suffered, but she'd never had her heart broken. Never felt that slap of rejection when everything you thought you knew about somebody turned out to be a pack of lies. He hoped she never would – because it meant you could never quite see relationships in the same way again.

"I'm not sure what she fell in love with, to be honest. Or what I fell in love with, either. I was different then...and if I'm honest, I think Johanna was part of a lifestyle deal. I had the big job. The flash car. The social life. When I met her she seemed perfect and I fell in love with her. Or at least I thought I did. Now – and believe me, you get a lot of thinking time in prison – I think I fell in love with idea of her, of us. We worked as a couple. She fitted my profile just as much as I fitted hers. It's entirely possible I was just as shallow as she was."

"I don't believe that for a minute," said Pippa, wrinkling her nose up in a scowl. "If the roles had been reversed, you'd have stuck by her, wouldn't you?"

"I've thought about that one a lot, funnily enough," he replied. "And yes, I would. But she didn't stick by me, and this was the woman I intended to spend the rest of my life with – which says a lot about my taste in women, doesn't it? Anyway. Enough. That's water under the bridge. She's gone and since then there's not been anyone else. Even though I did get a few marriage proposals from women in their fifties while I was in jail, as well as the occasional man. Strangely enough I wasn't tempted – and I can't see it ever happening now. Me and women are a thing of the past."

"Well that's just silly," she said, frowning at him. "How can you say that? You're only young. You can't condemn yourself to being single for the rest of your life just because of one dud. You might meet someone else – someone wonderful."

"I might," he agreed, nodding. "But I don't think I could ever trust anyone else. And without that, really, what do I have to offer? Like I said, I'm no prize. Flirting – and it's been very nice, thank you – is as far as it goes for me and the fairer sex, at least at this stage."

There was a beat, a pause, as they both weighed up the statement he'd just made. It was a declaration, of sorts. A line that they couldn't – shouldn't – cross. A statement of intent for both of them.

"What a shame," Pippa replied, chewing her lower lip, thoughtfully. "And here was me, imagining the two of us going at it like bunny rabbits for the rest of the afternoon."

She was joking. He knew she was joking. But parts of him weren't so convinced.

This wasn't going to be the most relaxing holiday he'd ever had.

Chapter 6

Pippa was trying, to no avail, to shave her legs. But as this involved having a bath on her own, and getting at least ten minutes' peace and quiet, it wasn't going according to plan. Scotty was at the other end of the tub squirting her face with a water pistol and the twins were perched on the edge, fascinated by her unfamiliar actions.

"But why are you doing that?" asked Daisy, staring at her big sister's legs. "And why do you keep cutting yourself?" added Lily, poking one finger at her.

"Mainly because someone keeps prodding me!" snapped Pippa, deciding to give up. She'd managed one. The other would just have to stay forested. And anyway, they were right – there was no reason to be doing it. It's not like she'd be entering the North Cornish Miss Lovely Legs contest any time soon, or be prancing round in a mini skirt.

She climbed out and dried herself off, leaving Scotty to play for a few more minutes. He gave her a final squirt on the bum as she bent over to pick up the towel, much to everyone's amusement. At least she'd managed to wash her hair, she thought, and was now going to actually blow-dry it. Chores be damned! She was turning into a wild reckless fool!

Lily and Daisy looked on as she got dressed – in actual clean clothes with no holes in them – and even dabbed on a bit of blusher and lip gloss. She looked in the mirror and felt...odd. It hadn't been a lot of effort, but it had made a big difference. She felt like a different human being. A female one.

"You look like Cinderella," said Daisy, reaching up to touch Pippa's long blonde hair in awe. "And Ben can be Prince Charming!" added Lily, giggling. They were only little, but they'd already picked up on the difference, thought Pippa. The difference in her.

It was worrying because she felt it herself, this subtle change. Since their lunch in the pub, they'd settled into a steady routine. Ben had extended his stay for another week, and for the last nine days, he had got up early to help them with the animals, and even found a few jobs to do around the farm.

They'd carried on flirting, looking but not touching, and it had been...well, it had been lovely. They left the deep and meaningful stuff alone, and instead simply enjoyed it when their routines threw them together.

Despite her protests, he claimed he enjoyed being her odd-job slave, that a bit of manual labour helped his creative juices run more freely in the evening when he was writing. And watching him, moving with the easy grace of the very fit, she had to admit it got her juices flowing as well. Not necessarily creative ones. She'd never thought of watching a man replace rusty gate hinges as entertaining before, but this was better than a trip to the multi-screen. She found herself keeping one eye out of the window, noticing his hulking figure pottering around, hoping for a heatwave so he'd have to do it all without a shirt.

She was shameless, she thought, with a final peek in the mirror. But she was enjoying it, despite her doubts. She'd never had a man in her life before, beyond the postman and her own father all those years ago, and knowing he was around made her feel secure. Hopeful. And ever so slightly concerned.

Because what happened when he went? He'd been here less than a fortnight, yet somehow he'd become part of all their lives. He'd already been here longer than either of them had anticipated, and she wasn't the only one who'd got used to having him around. She might be the one putting on the lip gloss – but the kids had been affected as well. They enjoyed spending time with him, and she often caught Scotty sitting by his side, passing him tools and chatting to him.

Now, though, he only had two nights of his stay left. Then he'd go back to London and she'd go back to normality. Back to doing everything on her own. Back to having nobody to talk to, no adult company. Patrick's behaviour had improved since he'd started visiting Mr Jensen – she even had the sneaking suspicion he was starting to enjoy it – but he hardly qualified as an adult. Not in the way that Ben did.

It was all going to end – this brief interlude that had turned into as much of a holiday for her as it had for Ben. And that made her sad.

There was no fairy godmother and no glass slipper – or even a glass wellie. When Prince Charming left in his carriage they'd quite possibly never see him again. His life would move on – she had no doubt that he'd be famous for his books as well as his brawn before long. Everything would be different for him. But for them, it would be the same – but with a Prince Charming-shaped hole.

Huh. Prince Charming. She hoped they didn't mention that one when he came to dinner tonight. She'd die of embarrassment. Because while there was still a gentle air of flirtation between them, it was nothing more than that. She didn't have time for a man and he had made his feelings on the subject very clear – he was a woman-free zone.

Tonight, though, he was coming for dinner. It had been Scotty's idea, bizarrely. The four-year-old had taken to Ben in a way she'd never seen him react before. He'd followed him around on his "jobs", passing him tools like a surgeon's assistant. Playing football with him in the field. Asking for him as soon as he woke.

On the one hand it was a joy to see him open up, but on the other...again, worrying. Because Ben would be leaving. Ben wasn't his father. Ben wasn't her boyfriend. Ben most definitely wasn't Prince Charming. Ben wasn't going to be around for the hard times, when Scotty was crying in the night, and Patrick was drunk, and she was shovelling snow off the driveway. Ben was temporary, and she needed to be one hundred percent okay with that.

Which is exactly why, she thought, spraying a bit of perfume on her wrists, she was taking so much care getting ready for a chicken-casserole dinner in her own kitchen. Duh.

"You look really pretty, Pippa," said Scotty, ambling towards her, naked and soaking wet. Since when had he learned to climb out of the bath on his own? He was growing so fast she could barely keep up.

"Thank you very much, sweetie," she said, wrapping him in a towel and getting him dressed. What would happen to her when he grew up and left home? Her baby boy? Well, she thought, giving him a kiss on his damp blonde curls, she'd just have to go out and get a life of her own. She'd only be in her thirties, after all. Hardly ancient. There'd be time for love later on. She might meet someone wonderful. After all, she'd pretty much given Ben a pep talk on exactly the same subject that day at the pub, so she should at least do herself the same kindness.

As soon as he heard the knock on the door and the sound of the latch lifting, Scotty wriggled out of her grasp – luckily dressed apart from one missing sock – and was out of her arms and down the stairs. She heard Daisy and Lily thundering after him.

"Pippa!" Daisy cried. "Prince Charming is here!"

She grimaced and scooped up the wet towels Scotty had left on the bedroom floor. So much for being a princess – there was always going to be laundry to do and no magic woodland creatures to do it for her...

Slinging the towels in the basket, she patted her silky hair down one last time and went downstairs. Ben was standing in the kitchen, acting as a human climbing frame for all three kids, who were draped strategically over his shoulders, back and legs. Once he'd managed to shake them all off, he turned round with a smile.

Prince Charming indeed, she thought, feeling that now-familiar hitch in her breathing. He'd dressed up too and was wearing a crisp, pale-blue shirt that made his skin look even more tanned. His hair was freshly washed and she swore she could still smell his shower gel – something spicy and male and expensive and utterly lush. His head was slightly stooped, as though avoiding the beams in the ceiling, and he was holding out a bunch of wild flowers that had obviously been picked from her own meadow.

The man was completely edible, and she worried for a moment that she might actually be drooling. Maybe it was a good thing he'd be leaving soon – she wasn't sure her libido could take much more. After years of giving men little or no thought at all, she now found she couldn't go more than a few minutes without thinking about him. Imagining putting her hands on his shoulders, tiptoeing up, and placing a great big smacker on those luscious lips of his. Slipping her hands under whatever clothing he was wearing and exploring the magnificent torso she knew lay beneath it.

It was way too distracting, and starting to chip away at a sense of independence she never even realised she had. Him being here was changing her and she wasn't convinced she wanted that at all.

"I brought you these," he said, holding out the bouquet, his smile chasing away all her vague anxieties. "I realise that technically picking them from your meadow was theft, but I hope you'll forgive me. You look...beautiful."

Pippa smiled, absurdly pleased that he'd noticed.

"Thank you. Just goes to show how bad I normally look," she replied, taking the flowers and sniffing them as she placed them in a vase. "Please, sit down – dinner's almost ready. I think Patrick may even be gracing us with his presence."

"How's it going with him and Mr Jensen?" he asked, seating himself at the table. He immediately started refereeing as the children squabbled about who got to sit next to him. She was about to step in, then realised he'd sorted the situation out already, with a few simple comments and the setting up of a rota system. He was good with them, she thought. Maybe a bit too good.

Shaking off that slight feeling of unease, she served up dinner, hearing Patrick's gentle footfall thudding down the stairs, shaking the whole room like an approaching giant. He even had to stoop his head as he came through the door.

"Ask him yourself," she replied. "He's obviously smelled food."

Patrick – washed, shaved and looking almost like a normal human being, demolished two bowls of casserole, all the time telling them about Mr Jensen, his life and especially his time in North Africa during the war. She couldn't remember the last time he'd been so animated, and he wasn't even drunk. He'd even been going back there voluntarily – and thankfully without Robbie – just to "help out the old geezer". She was starting to think that him trashing Mr Jensen's garden was one of the best things that had ever happened to him, and prayed that it was the rock bottom he needed to hit before he crawled back up.

"It sounds really cool, sis," he said, mopping up the gravy with a chunk of home-made bread. "I know it was a war and all, but it sounds like they had a right laugh as well. I was thinking that maybe the army life might be for me..."

There was a lull in the conversation, and Pippa felt a chill run up and down the small hairs on her arms. Patrick? In the army? Shipped off to Iraq or God knows where? Given a real-life gun? She must have looked as horrified as she felt, because he immediately burst out laughing.

"Only kidding – just wanted to see your face! Actually, I was thinking about applying to agricultural college next year. I know my grades aren't brilliant – okay, they're really crap – but maybe

I could resit my exams. What do you think? Mr Jensen thinks it's a good idea. Says he'll even give me a reference."

Pippa paused, spoon midway to her mouth, and the whole family stared at her.

"Could you please tell me when the alien invasion came and what they've done with the real Patrick?" she asked, standing up to clear the dishes. "I think it's a great idea! If you need any help with the application – "

"Yeah, like filling the whole thing in!"

"– then you know where I am. Right, I'm going to put the kids to bed."

There was an immediate protest, as all three of the children claimed they wanted Ben to read them their bedtime stories.

Again, she felt it – the slight raising of hackles. She liked Ben – maybe more than that – and the kids adored him. He'd been nothing but honest and open and gentle with her. He'd helped around the farm, he'd played with Scotty, he'd made time for Patrick when everyone else, including her, was ready to give up on him. But he was, she reminded herself again, only temporary. Was it right to let him this close, to let him read them bedtime stories, let him become such a favourite in their lives? And was it even them she was worried about, or just herself?

Life had been tough for the last few years, but she'd survived. She'd survived by coping alone. And now she felt all of that starting to crumble – it wasn't only the kids who looked forward to seeing him every day, it was her as well.

Patrick saved her from making a decision by stepping in.

"Nah. I'm putting you all to bed," he said. "And then I'm going to play *Call of Duty* on the X-Box till my eyes bleed. Sis and Ben can go out for a drink or something. Grown-up stuff."

The children grumbled until he started chasing them, pretending he was a zombie while he pursued them up the stairs, making them shriek in delight. Pippa looked on in amazement – she couldn't remember the last time Patrick had voluntarily done anything for someone else, especially her. She was normally enemy number one. Either aliens really had invaded or Patrick was showing signs of growing up. If you'd asked her a month ago, she'd have sworn that a close encounter of the ET kind was the more likely of the two.

She turned to Ben, still holding the tea towel in her hands. He smiled, seeming to sense her tension.

"Well, do you fancy it?" he asked.

"What?" she replied, her imagination stepping in to fill a few gaps. This was crazy. One minute she wanted to shoo him out of her nest for getting too close, the next she wanted to lick his face. Maybe she was going insane.

"A drink. A walk. Skinny-dipping in the bay."

All of the above and more, she thought. He might only be here for a few more days – maybe she should make the most of them.

Chapter 7

Barrelstock Bay was one of Pippa's very favourite places in the whole world – which was lucky, as it was only a couple of miles away from the farm.

It was almost always deserted, thanks mainly to the fact that you needed a hefty four-wheel drive and nerves of steel to get to it. At night, in particular, it was rare to see another living soul. Unless you counted the nervous foxes and shrews you occasionally saw illuminated in car headlights, dashing away from the road the minute anyone approached.

The beach was made up of pebbles and rocks of all shapes and sizes, washed smooth by millennia of waves, interspersed with patches of fine yellow sand. On both sides, the sea crashed into cliffs that had been hewn into haggard shapes by the constant ebb and flow of the ocean. The moonlight filtered through the cove, dappling the sand and rocks, casting the whole bay in an eerie glow.

She wasn't sure why she'd brought him here, to this special place. A place she almost held as sacred and had visited alone so many times in the last few years. It had been her secret haven, a hideaway she fled to when she needed time to regroup. It wasn't unheard of for her to come straight here after a particularly fraught school run, and spend hours talking herself down off the edge of her I-Can't-Do-This cliff. Hopefully not out loud or the foxes might grass her up to Social Services.

She came here on the anniversary of her parents' death and on their birthdays. For the last few years on her birthday as well – because nobody was throwing her a party and baking a cake any time soon. She'd spent her twenty-first here, with nothing but the ocean for company, and it hadn't been anywhere near as sad as it sounded. Because when she was sitting on the sand at Barrelstock Bay, she was at peace.

Maybe that's why she brought him here – why she thought he'd understand and love it as much as she did. They both needed some peace and that's what she associated the Bay with. Peace and fun and happiness. And now, with Ben. With this virtual stranger, who had somehow found a place in her home, in the children's lives, and, she was beginning to suspect, in her poor befuddled heart.

The night was mild, but they were both huddled beneath the blanket she'd brought with them from the Land Rover. A flask of hot coffee sat at their feet and for a while they were both silent, listening to the sound of the waves and the scurrying of small animals in the scrubby bushes behind them.

"Why does this blanket smell of dog when you don't have a dog?" said Ben, breaking the quiet. "And why don't you have a dog, anyway? I'd expect a border collie called Postman Pat or something."

"Ah. You must have been a detective in a previous life," replied Pippa. "This was the blanket we always kept in the car when we took Leonardo out with us."

"Leonardo? A dog named after a famous artist?"

"No, stupid. A dog named after a Teenage Mutant Ninja Turtle – and a lab, not a collie. It's a bit of a family tradition, letting kids choose the names. He died last year, which was fair enough as he was about a thousand in doggie years, and I just haven't had the heart to get rid of it. I don't even notice the smell any more. Sorry if it's a bit gross."

"No, not gross at all. Just dog, nothing wrong with that. Could be worse. Could be Harry Potter...smells are so powerful aren't they? One whiff of something evocative and it's as if your mind jumps into a time machine."

For him, he knew, that wasn't so good. The smell of over-boiled veg would forever remind him of prison meals. The smell of Opium would forever remind him of Johanna – the one she always wore. But maybe, he pondered, subtly inhaling the aroma floating up from Pippa's cloud of pale hair, they could be replaced. With something new, something better.

The smell of lavender shampoo, for instance, would now be forever pinned in his olfactory memory. Maybe he'd start visiting lavender farms or herbalists just to bring back this moment, to bring back these images. Because right here, right now, he felt more content than he had for years. Possibly forever. He'd eaten a delicious home-cooked meal in a family kitchen, with a family that had welcomed him. He was looking at one of the most beautiful views he'd ever seen. And sitting right next to him, beneath a blanket that smelled of a long-gone lab, was Pippa. He knew it couldn't last – that real life would come along and punch him on the hooter before too long – but just in that one moment, everything felt right. More than right. Perfect.

"It's breathtaking, isn't it?" she murmured, nestling her slim figure closer to his.

"What? The eau de Leonardo? It's not that bad..."

She poked him, sharply, in the ribs, and he made a noise that sounded suspiciously like a little girl squealing.

"No, you idiot – the bay. It's magic, you know."

"Really? Like pixies?"

"Maybe, although I've never seen any myself. Apart from that unfortunate incident with the absinthe...I wish. Anyway. Even without pixies, for me, it's magic. It was a smuggler's cove back in the day, and I always think if I close my eyes, I can still see it – the wrecked boats, the lanterns, the barrels of brandy floating in on the waves. It's so quiet now, but then it must have been a hive of activity. Or maybe I've just been watching *Poldark* a bit too much."

Ben paused, closed his eyes, willed himself to see what Pippa saw, to picture the vivid scenes she conjured up.

"No. You're right," he said after a moment. "It is magic. I wish we had some of that brandy right now. The wind's getting up... are you warm enough?"

She was, she thought, but snuggled closer all the same. The feel of his solid, warm presence next to her was swamping her senses. Their hips touching; their thighs leaning against each other. His arm around her shoulder, holding her close, keeping her safe. It was bliss and she never wanted it to end. She knew it was an illusion, but it was a wonderful one. The bay never let her down.

"I'm fine," she replied. "I always am when I'm here. This is where our parents used to bring us on holiday. I know it's only a few miles away, but there was never enough money or time for trips abroad or theme parks or any of that stuff. So we used to come here – with a little camping stove and some sausages. Marshmallows on sticks. Ghost stories – the whole deal. They had a camper van, one of those old VW things that ran forever. It was three colours – blue, white and rust – but it got us here."

"I just about remember coming here on my own with them, before Patrick was born, and it carried on all the way until...well, until they died. It was just...our place. Every memory I have of this bay is perfect, and if I close my eyes again, I can almost see them as well – laughing and playing, mum burning the sausages and dad skimming stones and Leonardo eating the marshmallows. Happy. All of us together. I wish they were still here, but I know I was lucky to have had them at all. And this is the place I still feel them the most, like they're still here, watching over me. Telling me they love me, and to buck my ideas up. When I'm down, it brings me back up – and when I'm up, I come here to celebrate it. With them."

"Then it really is magic," he said, leaning in to kiss the top of her head. "And I'm honoured that you brought me here. Thank you for sharing it with me, and thank you for the last week or so. There's been a sprinkling of pixie dust over my whole time here, don't you think? Or is it always like this?"

"No, it's not – the pixies have definitely been busy. We've loved having you around, Ben, and we'll all be sad to see you go on Tuesday. Maybe you'll come back and see us again some time when you're a famous author. Give me some notice and I'll even make sure the toilet's working."

Her tone was calm and even. Resigned. He wondered if that was how she felt – if he was just another guest among the dozens who stayed at Honeysuckle Cottage every year? If she'd wave him goodbye, then go back to her everyday life as though they'd never met? Move on to her next visitors, show them the sights, bake them fresh bread, bring them to this magical place as well?

For some reason, the thought made his heart seize up, as if someone had slammed him with a defibrillator. The thought of leaving all this behind: the countryside, the sea, the wildflower meadows. Of going back to London, to his pristine flat crammed full of bad memories. Back to avoiding eye contact on the Tube and getting jostled in the supermarket as the worker ants foraged for food. Mainly, if he was honest, the thought of leaving Pippa – her soft laughter, her strength, her lavender hair. He'd made so many vows about himself and women. Himself and people, in fact. But now he was finding it hard to imagine his everyday life without her and the kids and even the bloody animals. This was meant to be a holiday – but now it felt like a new reality. A much better one. They'd found a chink in his armour and snuck through it without even trying. It was frightening and wondrous all at the same time.

"Well, what if I don't go back?" he said. "What if I stay a bit longer? I'm getting lots of work done here. Nobody bothers me. I could stay. If that was all right with you."

He paused, all his senses on hyper-alert. Waiting for her to say no, waiting for her body to tense up next to his. Waiting for the rejection he always seemed to expect since Johanna had done her walking routine. Waiting for her to shove him right off this dream cloud and back into reality.

"That would be...all right with me," she murmured, after what felt like a lifetime. "I have a booking, but I could move them into Primrose, as long as I could get the dishwasher working again."

"I can fix dishwashers," he added quickly, feeling his heart beat faster. Calm down, you idiot, he thought. All she's said yes to is taking your money for another week or so. This isn't your life and it never will be. You're on borrowed time. You're a paying guest, and maybe a friend, and perhaps she fancies you just a little bit. But nothing more than that – and certainly nothing that merited this kind of hyperventilation.

"Of course you can fix dishwashers. You're Ben Retallick. You can do anything. But I was wondering..." she said, her fingers creeping onto his thighs. "...if this was enough for you? Staying here, like this? I know you've sworn off all contact with womenfolk etc. etc., but...well, there has been that pixie dust, hasn't there? Maybe I'm imagining it, but there seems to be something more between us, Ben. More than I'd like there to be, maybe, but I think it's there. I'm not the world's most experienced of women, but when we're together, it feels...kind of yummy."

"You're not imagining it, Pippa. And yummy is exactly the right word. *But...*" he said, distracted by the touch of her soft fingers on his legs, the sensations that were coursing through him. He couldn't even hear the sea, his heart was pounding so fast. A pterodactyl could fly overhead carrying a cow and all he'd notice was the fact that she was stroking him, and his body was reacting in an immediate and disconcerting way.

This, he thought, was right where he should stop it. Move her hand and end it. This is where he should draw the line. At flirtation, at fun, at friendship.

But her hand was still moving, running up and down his thigh, and he could hear her breath, coming faster than it had any right to come. He could smell her hair and feel the outline of her breast as she leaned closer in to him. He was barely capable of thought, never mind drawing lines and sticking to them. Any line he drew right now was likely to be pretty wonky.

"But what?" she asked, fingertips skimming over his groin, her eyes widening as she felt him there; felt the reaction her touch had provoked.

"But...God, how do you expect me to think when you're doing that? I'm only flesh and blood, you know! No, Pippa, you're not imagining it. It's quite obvious that you're not imagining it."

He nuzzled her hair, inhaled the scent of her, gave himself over to the pleasure of feeling a soft, sweet woman cuddled next to him. It had been so long...

"I feel it too," he said. "I want you so much it drives me crazy. I sit in that cottage every night picturing you in bed, wanting to join you. I see you around the farm and I want you. I even see you in your wellies, carrying shovels full of pig manure, and I still want you. I didn't expect this, not ever. You're way too young for me. You're way too good for me. I know all of that and I still want you."

"You're thinking too much," she replied, turning her face to look up into his eyes. "And you're talking too much. Let me come back to Honeysuckle with you, tonight. We may never get the opportunity again, and I want you too. I'm so sick of denying myself everything I want. It's been so hard, for so long, and... Lord, I don't want to sound like a L'Oréal advert, but I'm worth it. I deserve it! I deserve some fun, for mollusc's sake! Even if it's just for one night, I deserve to forget everything I have to do, everything I need to accomplish. I want to forget about tax bills and chores and Social Services and Patrick.

"For one night, I want to forget about all of my responsibilities, about everything apart from the way you make me feel. I know this isn't forever, Ben, for either of us. We both have our reasons for that – pretty good reasons. But for now, I'd like to just be...a woman. Not a mother, or a sister, or a bloody plumber. Just a woman. Can you help me with that?"

He looked down at her, at those huge eyes reflecting the moonlight, at the hair pooling around her shoulders, and realised that resistance was futile. He was a dead man walking.

"There's nothing I'd like better," he said. "Now where are the car keys?"

She'd been steady and focused on the drive back, concentrating ferociously on the road despite the hormones raging inside her. Ever since her parents had died, driving had been something she'd taken very seriously, and even the presence of Ben and all his man-bits sitting next to her didn't alter that.

The minute he unlocked the door to Honeysuckle Cottage, though, that all changed. She'd expected to feel shy, nervous, uncertain. Because she was capable of being all of those things, especially as she'd just propositioned a man for the first time in her life.

Instead, it was as though her inner slut had been unleashed, and she practically threw herself at him the minute the door quietly clunked shut behind them.

He barely had time to breathe before she draped her arms around his neck, reaching up on tiptoes to kiss him. He leaned back against the door, scooped her up so her legs wrapped around his waist, clinging on to him.

He kissed her back, hard and hot, and it was everything she'd wanted it to be: urgent and fast and needy. She could feel the musculature of his shoulders beneath her hands, and the press of his erection against her, and wanted more, immediately. Even kissing him, even being held tight against him, was breathtaking – like nothing she'd ever encountered.

"Slow down, Pippa," he said, pulling his lips away from hers, smiling when he saw her expression. A child who'd had her latest toy taken off her. Pouting and sulky, lips swollen and red.

He stroked her hair from the sides of her face, leaned in to trace her cheekbones with his lips, dropped lower and gently kissed the hollow of her throat. She sighed and rubbed herself against him, dragging his t-shirt up so she could make contact with bare skin.

"Slow down...we have all night," he said, nipping at the sensitive flesh of her neck, "if you want to feel like a woman, then let me take my time – let me make this special for you."

"I'm sorry," she sighed, leaning her head on his shoulder, hands still playing over the smooth skin of his back. "I'm not very experienced, and I'll probably be rubbish, and I've basically been imagining this ever since you got here."

"There's no need to be sorry," he replied, pulling her face back so he could meet her eyes, kissing her softly, slowly. "And you won't be rubbish – I'll take enthusiasm over skill any day. But I don't want to rush this. I've been imagining it too – and there's a whole week's worth of sexual fantasy stored up in my brain waiting to come out and play...now let me take you to bed. Let me make you forget everything you want to forget."

Her cornflower eyes were clouded with desire and she was chewing on her full lower lip. Her hair was splayed around her head like gold dust and she shook her head sadly.

"I already have," she said. "What's your name again?"

Chapter 8

"You look happy, sis – late night playing Scrabble, was it?" asked Patrick, as he ambled into the kitchen. The gravel scars on his face were healing up and it looked suspiciously as if he'd just had his second shower in as many days. Miracles, she thought, would never cease.

She ignored his comment – sarcasm, she'd always been told, was the lowest form of wit – and instead handed him a mug of steaming tea. She hadn't even spat in it. She was that happy.

Happy and tired, and aching in places she never even knew she had. Ben had made her forget, all right – she'd forgotten everything but the touch of his long, strong fingers, the lick of his tongue, the glorious sight of his naked body. The way he'd made her murmur his name, over and over. The way he'd made her feel things she'd never known it was possible to feel. The way he'd taken her body to a strange and foreign land, full of delights and pleasures and delicious pains. She'd been busily thinking "wow", replaying it all in her mind, ever since she'd got up, and suspected the smile would never leave her face. The mums had stared at her when she'd done the school run and she knew she must look exactly like what she was: a woman who'd spent a very good night with a very bad man. It had been...amazing, all of it.

None of which, she thought, Patrick needed to know. He may be a grown-up, but he'd always be her baby brother. She'd never had a sex life before, and it would be great to have someone to talk to about it, but Patrick was most definitely not that person. Even if the smug grin on his big, daft face told her he knew exactly what she'd been up to, and was most amused by it. It probably made a change for someone else in the family to be the naughty one.

"Do you really want me to answer that question?" she said, raising her eyebrows at him. "Or would you prefer it if I drew you some diagrams?"

He laughed and she was taken aback by the sound of it. She didn't think she'd heard Patrick laugh for...well, three years or so. Her heart swelled with love and affection: for so long, she'd looked at him and only seen trouble. Thought of him and only felt anxiety. Spoken to him like a shrew instead of someone who cared about him. How had that felt for him? To know he was the thorn in her side, the millstone around her neck? It can't have been easy, playing the bad boy for all this time, when she knew he was an essentially decent person. Maybe it was time for them both to change, not just him.

"I love you, Patrick," she said abruptly, which wiped the smile right off his face.

"Er...yeah. I know that. Thanks, sis, but let's not get carried away, eh? We are English, you know? Too much of that lovey-dovey stuff and I'll be sick in my mouth. Right. I'm off to do some gardening. D'you want me to drop the kids off at school or something?"

"Thanks for the offer," she said, clearing the cups away, "but they've already been there for two hours. Your body clock doesn't seem to run to the same time table as the rest of us, does it?"

"Guess not. Laters. Don't do anything I wouldn't do..."

As Patrick was, she knew, already something of a legend amongst the teenaged girls of the village, she suspected that left her with a lot of leeway.

She finished rinsing the dishes, then poured two fresh mugs of coffee. She'd already deposited the kids at school, done the morning feed and replied to her emails. And, she added with a wry smile, found time to brush my hair, iron a clean t-shirt, and track down underwear that actually matched. A red-letter day indeed.

She walked out into the courtyard, pausing to enjoy the feel of sunlight on her face. The grey clouds had finally cleared and the air positively hummed with summer. She could hear the gulls over the bay; the sound of honeybees in the hedgerows, lambs bleating in the fields. It was warm – it was bright. It was fan-bloody-tastic.

She'd woken up in her own bed – much as she enjoyed making love with Ben, she still had some responsibilities she couldn't forget – and listened as Scotty pattered down the hallway towards her. He'd climbed in, bleary-eyed, hair tangled and immediately asked when he could see Ben. That had been the norm for the last week and for the first time she found her own heart echoing it. She knew she'd said it was only for one night, and maybe it was – but as soon as she was conscious, she'd found herself thinking about him again. He filled her mind and smothered all sanity. It was terrifying and terrific, and totally new to her.

Any minute now, she thought, I'll make time to start worrying about that...

"What can you see up there that I can't?" said Ben, emerging from Honeysuckle to find her standing dead still, holding two mugs of coffee, face turned up to stare at the sky. The sun streamed down around her, glinting off her hair, making her look like some pastoral angel fallen to earth. Wearing a Simpsons t-shirt.

She gave him a grin that could crack the hardiest of souls and he felt a little bit of himself cry for help.

Ben had woken up that morning alone, tangled in sheets that had seen some heavy-duty action the night before. He was supposed to have been the one showing her the sexual ropes, but in reality, she'd blown his mind. Her sensuality, her abandon, the totally wanton side of her nature that had emerged and taken complete control.

There was no pretence, no coyness, no game-playing: just one hundred percent joyous lust. One night with Pippa, he'd decided, was worth a lifetime with any other woman.

He'd slept late, exhausted, reaching out for her as soon as he started to swim back to consciousness. Stretching his arm out over the pillow, he'd found her gone and fought back a moment of panic. A moment where he felt the same blind emptiness that had consumed him after Johanna had left. Default setting: she's done a runner.

Well, Pippa wasn't Johanna, he reminded himself. She couldn't be more different if he'd designed them himself. And more importantly, they'd made no promises to each other – no promises made meant that none could be broken, and he could set aside that panic, that fear. This was a completely different situation.

One night, Ben Retallick, he told himself. One night to make Pippa forget. To make yourself forget. One night, that's all.

What had he expected? For her to be there, wearing a negligee and presenting him with a gin and tonic? To be so awe-struck by his skills in the sack that she fell madly in love with him?

No, none of that...but it had still hurt, more than he cared to admit, to wake up without her. He'd rolled over, sniffed the pillow, gone immediately hard at the faint traces of lavender on the linen. Groaned with frustration and headed straight for a cold shower.

And now here she was, all things bright and beautiful, showering in sunshine and bearing coffee. Maybe it was all some kind of crazy dream: he'd wake up any minute in his prison bunk, listening to the shouts and yells of the other inmates, his nostrils assaulted by the smell of hundreds of trapped men instead of lavender shampoo. One hour in a concrete exercise yard instead of a whole day in a Cornish summer.

"I can see all kinds of things, Ben Retallick," she replied, squinting up at his face, still smiling, oblivious to his inner turmoil. "Things you city types can only imagine."

She walked towards him and he noticed she was wearing a bra today. A bra that did all kinds of pushy-up things to her breasts. Not that he had any complaints about them unfettered, but the underwear thing was already distracting...he wondered what colour it was, if there was any lace involved, whether the panties matched. How quickly he could get it off. If he should be heading straight back inside for another cold shower.

"Sorry I did a runner last night – I needed to be at home ready for Scotty's crack-of-dawn wake-up call. He'd freak out if I wasn't there. I meant to leave you a note, but I'd lost the use of my fingers, not to mention several other body parts. All your fault. How are you this morning?" she asked, placing the mugs of coffee down on the cobbles.

She moved to stand close to him, so close their bodies skimmed. She reached up, dragged her fingers into his hair, moved her hips forward so she was crushed in to him, her lips inches away from his.

"I'm...already turned on, you witch," he replied, clasping her even closer to him, burying his face in her hair. He kissed the side of her neck, already knowing the secret places that made her weak, and smiled to himself as she started to sigh, to sag, to writhe against him.

Pippa ran her hands over the breadth of his shoulders, down the ridged muscle of his back, slipped them under his top. She would never, in a million years, get tired of the way his body felt beneath her fingers. Iron abs wrapped in velvet skin, the jut of angular hip bones, the firm curve of his prize-winning backside. The feel of his erection trapped in the denim of his jeans, screaming how much he wanted her. That it might have been a one-night-only deal, but nobody had told his body that yet. It made her feel powerful, like some kind of earth goddess, that this Adonis of a man wanted her so much. That even with her messy hair, torn jeans and only one shaved leg, she could make him so hard so quickly.

"Yes, I can sense that," she said, rubbing herself shamelessly against him like a purring cat. "And believe me, if I had one of those, it'd probably be in exactly the same state."

"I have other ways of telling, you know," he replied, snaking one hand up inside her t-shirt. "Secret ways."

He slipped her breast free of the bra cup, rolled his fingers around one taut bud of nipple until it was rigid beneath his touch. "Like that."

She moaned and the sound was like a heavenly choir singing into his ear: he could take her, right here, right now, out in the courtyard and she wouldn't stop him. She wanted him to, he could tell from the way her body moved, from the fast rhythm of her breath, the sharp scratch of her nails against his skin. She wanted him just as much this morning as she had last night.

"We'd better start behaving ourselves," he murmured, pulling away slightly. "Or we might end up on Google Earth."

"I don't care," she replied, flashing him that wicked grin again. "The way I feel right now, I'd happily dance a naked rumba in front of the Queen. There are no kids here. No Patrick. And SpongeBob's been there, done that, believe me. She won't mind at all if you rip my clothes off with your teeth and bonk me senseless up against that old oak tree...or are you too tired? I know you're getting on a bit, Ben. I wouldn't want to over-exert you!"

"It'll be a cold day in hell when I don't have the energy to bonk you senseless, Pippa Harte, but don't we have other things to do this morning? Don't you have guests arriving? And don't I have a dishwasher to fix? I thought that was part of the deal."

"It was," she said, picking up her coffee and sipping it, her eyes starting to clear as she focused on the reality of the day ahead. "In fact it's the only reason I had sex with you, to avoid the plumbing bills. You know, I'd completely forgotten about the new arrivals – see what you've done to me? Filled my brain with all this orgasm stuff, turned me into a nymphomaniac. Okay. You're right. Things to do. Pick up your coffee and follow me."

He did as he was told, admiring the view of her cute bottom striding ahead of him as he went. There were worse things to be doing with his time, he supposed...

Within minutes, she'd abandoned him in the kitchen of Primrose Cottage. The layout was similar to his own, with an open-plan design, low-flying beams and chintzy curtains. He crouched down, started to inspect the dishwasher in question, hoping that he could, in fact, fix it after all. He'd feel stupidly emasculated if he couldn't. That or secretly get a plumber out here without telling her. Stealth cheating.

He spent half an hour tugging and pulling at the connecting pipes before he realised where the blockage was. Somebody had helpfully left an apple core in there and it had lodged itself firmly in the drainage hose. The whole unit was old and rusting and really needed replacing, but it would do for now.

It was dirty work and uncomfortable, lying contorted on the tiled floor with his hands in strange places at strange angles. If he'd wanted something to distract him, he'd found the perfect activity.

When he finally came up for air, Pippa was perched on the sofa, watching him. With a very naughty expression on her face.

"I thought you were changing the bedding?" he asked, sitting up on his knees and wiping his damp hands down on the thighs of his Levis.

"I was. I have, in fact. But I wanted to see how you were doing," she said. "Check you weren't reneging on our bargain. You look hot, Ben. Don't you think you'd feel better if you did that without your t-shirt on?"

She gave him a look of perfect fake-innocence, and he felt his jeans swell in response. If he'd been uncomfortable before, he felt even worse now. How long had she been sitting there watching him while he had his head buried in the dishwasher, legs sticking out, arse in the air? Long enough to have got a flush on her cheeks, that's for sure.

"Ah," he said, smiling. "I think I've seen this film before. The one where I'm the plumber and you're the bored housewife? Shouldn't there be some cheesy seventies music in the background?"

"I don't know what you mean, you pervert. I'm just looking out for your wellbeing. It's a hot day out there. You're a paying guest. I wouldn't want you passing out from heat stroke. Now take your top off."

He gripped the hem of the black jersey and slowly, slowly, raised it, dragging it inch by inch up over his stomach, his torso, his chest, and eventually all the way off. He threw it behind him with a flourish and it landed in the sink. Big Bad Burlesque Ben.

Pippa looked on, for once lost for words. His hair was all mussed up where he'd pulled off the top, and his eyes were rich, shining chocolate. His body was perfect: wide shoulders, rippling muscle, all defined curves and ridges, glistening with the gentle sheen of sweat he'd built up while he was working. The Levis were stretched taut over his thighs and even tighter over his groin.

"Now come here," he said.

She went.

Chapter 9

"So..." said Ben, stretching out under the old oak tree. He was topless again – she seemed to like to keep him like that – and luxuriating in the feel of the June sunshine seeping into his bare skin. "Did that live up to expectations? After all, you've had over a decade to imagine it..."

"Well," replied Pippa, who had reverted to childhood type and was completely naked, "it was certainly better without getting thrown in the duck pond at the end of it."

"There's time yet," he added, raising his eyebrows wickedly at her. "Although I have other ways of getting you wet these days..."

He turned on his side, ran one lazy hand over her breasts, smiling when her ever-reliable nipples perked up to say hello. She arched her back slightly, stretching up to meet even the most casual of touches. They'd only just finished, and she was already responding, ready to go again, he thought. Amazing. Mind-boggling. Brilliant. This wild, crazy girl, still running around the farm starkers, still shocking him beneath the old oak tree. Still driving him mad, for all kinds of reasons. Thankfully, at least, she'd given up on the camo paint and the war cries. That would be taking things to a whole different level.

Pippa rolled over, snuggled into him, her head on his chest. Blonde hair spilled all over him, and she hooked one lithe, tanned leg over his body. She nipped at his skin and he yelped lightly, then wrapped her tighter in his arms. He was grinning so much he thought his face might break in two. Sunbathing with a post-coital, totally naked hot chick. Life didn't get much sweeter.

"You're right, though. I've been waiting to do that for such a long time," she said, nuzzling her face into him. "Even when you were a mere eighteen years old, instead of the OAP you are now, I fancied you. Obviously I didn't really get the whole sex thing, but I knew I liked you. I was fascinated by you, in fact. So I jumped on your head, from those branches up there. This is historic, this oak tree. In terms of our relationship, I mean. It's the tree from whence I first jumped your bones. I have to say you smell better now...you ponged like a scrumpy press that day, I seem to remember."

"The same is equally true in reverse," he said. "You smelled of animal poo all the time back then. At least now you only smell like animal poo some of the time."

"I'd like to argue with that point, but it's true...God! This is nice, isn't it? Kids in school. All the other guests out and about. Sunshine and al fresco sex beneath our very special oak tree. I feel like doing a happy dance. We should mark the occasion, Ben. Maybe I'll carve our initials in the trunk later. I can hobble back here on my walking stick when I'm as old as you and reminisce about the good old days. The days when a handsome stranger called Ben Retallick rolled up here in an Audi and rocked my world."

"And where will I be then, do you think?"

"Oh, dead probably..." she said, laughing into his chest. "No, you'll be a world-famous best-selling author, living like a hermit on a remote island in the South Pacific. The one with that old turtle, you know? The only one of its kind left in the world. You and him. Together forever. Sipping daiquiris and skinny-dipping, sharing little turtle moments, watching the sunset. No sex, though, I'm afraid. You're not his type."

"That's not a terribly happy future, is it?" asked Ben. "What would I do for nookie? A man has needs, you know!" he said, slapping her lightly on the bare bottom. He watched as the flesh rippled slightly, and felt his cock stir again. He was going to need intravenous vitamins if this continued much longer.

"Don't blame me. You're the one who's sworn off all contact with women."

"Not *all* contact..." he said, tracing the curve of her golden hip with his fingertips. All of this outdoor sex had given them both fantastic all-over tans at least. "I seem to be having plenty of 'contact' with you."

"That's just sex, though, isn't it? I know you like the sex. I like the sex. No, actually, I *love* the sex. Can't get enough of the stuff. You might have noticed."

"I have. I thoroughly approve."

"But when we started this, we said one night only. It's now been almost two weeks of this. I'm not complaining – in fact I'd complain if it stopped. But, well...you made yourself pretty clear, Ben. That this isn't serious for you. That you don't want anything serious, ever again. That Johanna – officially the stupidest woman in the world, if you ask my opinion – has switched you off from all that. I don't expect anything more from you. And I certainly don't expect you to give up your life with the turtle for me. To give up anything for me, in fact. I know that's not part of the deal with you and me."

Ben held her tight, staying silent for a few moments while he mulled it over. When she put it like that, it sounded so...harsh. Cynical. It made him feel like he was using her, exploiting her, even though they'd both been honest about their feelings all the way through. The problem with feelings, though, was that they tended to change. Just as you got used to one, it morphed into something completely unrecognisable.

He couldn't argue with what she'd said. She was right, of course. He had said all of those things. And more to the point, he'd meant them. This was a fling, and one they'd both gone into with eyes wide open – although that didn't tend to be the dominant body part when it came to Pippa.

He'd liked her, fancied her, responded to her. Enjoyed spending time with her, admired her. And when she made him an offer he couldn't refuse – well, he hadn't refused. He'd challenge any other straight man not to have done the same in his shoes. Now, as she squirmed in his arms, all that lovely soft skin pressed up against him, he couldn't find it anywhere in his heart to regret it.

And for the last fortnight, there had been nothing to regret. Their one night only had turned into an extended run, by mutual consent. They'd had sex in Primrose, in Honeysuckle, in Foxglove. In his car. In her Land Rover. In the sea. On the beach. In Bottom Paddock. On a surf board. In the wildflower meadow. On one memorable occasion, in the bluebell woods, moments before the place had been invaded by a small army of ramblers complete with backpacks and flasks. And now, minutes ago, here under the historic oak tree.

Everywhere, in fact, apart from in the farmhouse. He hadn't asked why, and he hadn't pushed – he understood that the main house was for her and the children. He could visit, but he couldn't stay. With so many other love-making venues to explore, it hadn't really bothered him. He was addicted to her and didn't care where it happened, as long as it did.

Beside, she was right. Venturing into the farmhouse would make it more...real. More serious. More permanent. Which neither of them was ready for. And in his case, he probably wouldn't ever be.

The novelty, he kept telling himself, would wear off eventually. Like in a hundred years or so. Or when he had to go back to London. To his real life. The one he wasn't that convinced he wanted any more. He hadn't got a clue what he wanted – but hurting Pippa was definitely not on the list. Had her feelings changed? Had his? He was already struggling to imagine life without her, and that worried him – he'd vowed never to give anyone that kind of power over his emotions again. Having power over his libido was one thing – she'd already conquered that one. But anything more? Anything that could come close to stitching up the hole in his heart that Johanna had left? He wasn't sure that was possible.

"You've gone all quiet," she said, poking him in the tummy. "Have I offended you? I didn't mean to, Ben. You probably shouldn't listen to me. Especially not when I've just gone cross-eyed with sex. I'm not really thinking straight. I'm just rambling. Maybe you should kiss me to shut me up."

"That's a very tempting offer," he said, briefly brushing his lips against hers, "but maybe we should talk about this. I've been here for almost a month now. And it's been great, really great. But I've taken it for granted that you're happy with this arrangement. That you're happy with me being here, sharing this time with you, knowing it won't lead to anything else. At some point, I have to go home, and I want to know that you'll be all right when I do. That you and the kids will be okay without me. That I'm not doing anything here that is going to damage you in any way."

She sat up, grabbed for her bra and knickers, both of which were hanging decoratively from the lower branches of the oak tree.

"If there's no more loving to be had, I'll make myself decent," she said, snapping herself in place. He felt sad to see her lovely breasts hidden away again, but it was probably a sensible idea. Few men could think straight with a nice pair of boobs on display. She messed around for a while, taking a lot longer to get dressed than it usually took her. He suspected she was playing for time, stalling before she had to answer his question. She was probably as confused as he was.

"Come on," she said, holding out a hand to help him up. "Let's walk back to the farm. I collected some nice fresh eggs this morning, we can have them on toast for lunch. And yes, I'm sure I'll be fine when you go. Either I'll be fine or I'll have a nervous breakdown, but if I do it'll only be a very small one. I won't have time for anything dramatic."

She set off, fast, and he dashed to catch her, his longer legs eating up the distance. He grabbed hold of her hand, whirled her around to face him. He was horrified to see what looked like tears in her eyes. Tears that he'd put there by being a pushy bastard. By insisting they talk about things when she'd been perfectly content to ignore all the complexities and focus on the moment, the here and now. The incredibly perfect time they had been having together, until he went and put his foot in it.

"I'm sorry," she said, as he held her face gently in his long fingers, wiping away stray tears with the tips of his thumbs. "I'm being a complete rubber duck about this. It's just that I was about to do a happy dance and I was all floaty and loved-up, and then you – "

"Made you think about it all ending. It's me who should be sorry. We do need to talk, but only when you're ready. Only when you have something you want to say. Not just because I want to sort my head out, or assuage my potentially guilty conscience. Look, Pippa. I don't know what the hell is going on with us. This has become more than either of us expected it to, certainly more than I expected it to. And it's not just sex, is it? I know we intended it to be, but it's not, no matter how many times you or I say it is. We can't keep kidding ourselves – we're both in a lot deeper than we ever intended. In fact, I don't think it ever was just sex; there was always a connection there between us. And...and maybe I was naive to think we could ever escape this without collateral damage."

Her eyes flashed up at him and she smacked his hands away from her face.

"Escape it? Collateral damage? What language are you speaking, Ben? You're not in a courtroom now, and you're not in jail! Nobody is forcing you to be here, and there doesn't have to be damage at all! All this time I've thought this was what we both wanted, and then you go and say something like that? Are you already planning your great escape, then? Digging a tunnel all the way to the M5? Wondering if I'll sue you for emotional harm afterwards?

"You know what? You're impossible! I haven't got a clue what you want from me. You said you wanted sex, I gave you sex. I love giving you sex. You said you didn't want anything serious, I gave you light-hearted. Then when I'm busy being light-hearted and enjoying it, you go all heavy on me, acting like I'm going to commit suicide the minute you take your admittedly gorgeous arse back to London!

"I don't know what this is! I don't know what we're doing! I know you don't want anything long- term. I know I'm too messed up to even try it...so why can't it stay like this? It's so bloody... perfect! Why do we have to talk about it? Why do we have to consider the *collateral damage*? I know you'll be going. I know! And I don't want to think about it. I just don't! Maybe that's childish, but as you keep reminding me, I am only a child, aren't I?"

He wanted to hold her, to comfort her, but her anger was fizzing through her body so hard she was practically popping with it. And anyway, what could he say? What would make it better? There was truth in everything she said. Casual words had spilled from his damaged ego and he'd hurt her. Infuriated her. And he *was* impossible. He knew that. Pippa had never made a single demand on him – other than sexual – and had presented him with the perfect escape from real life. But now he was starting to wonder, at what cost, to both of them?

"I'm sorry, Pippa," he said, keeping his distance despite the fact that his fingers were twitching to touch her. "I'm sorry I spoiled the moment. I should have just let you do your happy dance. But all those things – about me, about my past – they're still true. I still don't feel ready for anything more."

"That," she replied, narrowing her eyes, hands on hips, "is perfectly obvious. And I'd like to point out, Ben Retallick, that I haven't even *asked* for anything more! Not once, you arrogant pig! Your head is so far up your own backside you can't see out – you're so worried about protecting your precious feelings, aren't you? All because one bitch of a woman screwed you over. Has it ever occurred to you that I'm not ready for more either? That I have my own doubts and fears? And not just because of me and the way I feel, but because I have an entire family to look out for? That I have a four-year-old who thinks you're cooler than Star Wars Lego and twin girls who have crushes on you the size of Pluto, and a teenaged oaf of a brother who looks up to you? That even without considering my own bloody emotional state, I have all of that to think about?

"You, Ben Retallick, can be a perfect moron sometimes – all I wanted was some fun. Some pleasure. I'm not some neurotic girl who's hoping to marry you. I know this isn't real. All I wanted was to enjoy the time we have left together – is that really so bad?"

She ran off down the hill, hair streaming behind her, bare feet padding through the long grass.

Ben stood where he was, knowing that she needed time to cool off. And he needed time to think. At least, he thought, wryly, I'm a perfect moron. If you're going to do something at all, at least do it well...

Pippa sat in the school assembly hall, her senses assaulted by the familiar smells of cooked dinners, PE lessons and cleaning fluids. No chalk these days, though, which she always thought was a shame.

She'd attended the same school until she was eleven, and sitting here, legs crossed, perched on one of the tiny plastic chairs, always made her feel about eight years old. As though she should be wearing her uniform and plaits and being careful not to run in the hallway. Some of the staff from her time were still here, in that timeless, ageless way that teachers have. They never had first names and they never existed outside the classroom. She still remembered the shock of seeing Mrs Clements in the local Tesco when she was little – she was convinced they all had camp beds set up at school and never left the building. School was a tiny, perfect world, totally self-contained.

Now, though, she was here as a grown-up. As a parent, despite the fact that she'd never given birth in her life. It was Consultation Night, and she was here to consult, waiting to meet the Reception class teacher who looked after Scotty. The twins were done and at least, she thought, she didn't have to deal with Patrick's teachers any more. Wow, that had been a barrel-load of laughs – walking into the local comprehensive that she'd only left the year before herself, listening to sympathetic teachers break the not-so-shocking news that her brother was unlikely to be getting a clean sweep of A-stars in his GCSEs. They'd meant well and tried to help, but it had still been awful. You shouldn't be going to parents' evenings at eighteen, you just shouldn't.

Now, a few years on, she was more accustomed to it. Didn't feel quite so squeamish as she wriggled on the baby chair. Felt a bit more able to ask questions without putting her hand up first.

Her meeting with the twins' teacher had gone well. They were communicating, playing with others, and they only reverted to their secret language when one of them was upset. All good news – apart from the fact that they'd both been telling Miss Rowley about their new friend. Their new friend who was really tall and loads of fun. The new friend they called Prince Charming. The bloody man was everywhere – there was no escape. Miss Rowley thought he was imaginary and Pippa did nothing to disabuse her. Maybe he was. A group hallucination.

She'd calmed down after her blow-up on the hill. And really, she was a bit embarrassed about it now. Everything she'd said – okay, yelled – had been true, but it was still embarrassing. Juvenile. She'd acted like an angry teenager, while Ben stayed so calm, so distant. So completely walled-off. He was obviously used to hysterical females and none of it had seemed to faze him. While she had steam pumping out of her ears, he'd stood there, watching and listening and refusing to be dragged into it.

She'd taken the sensible route and simply avoided him for the rest of the day. It wasn't as if she didn't have anything else to do. There were so many chores piling up – paperwork and housework, and the little DIY tasks that he'd been taking on without being asked. Her ironing pile was the size of Mount Vesuvius, and the shower needed unblocking, just for starters. With a houseful of hairy oiks, it always seemed to need it, and an hour on her hands and knees deconstructing some minor plumbing had been exactly what she needed to take her mind off things.

She'd been spending so much time with Ben, she knew, that she'd been neglecting her duties. Life had always been busy, and now she was fitting in several hours a day for sex and flirting as well. And as there were still only twenty-four available to her. It couldn't go on like this. A break from reality was fine for a few days, but this had been too long. Too long without focus, without her usual work ethic. Her usual routines and discipline. And if all those plates she was spinning over her head crashed to the ground, it wasn't just her life that descended into chaos – it was the kids' as well.

Finding out that the twins had taken their hero worship into school hadn't helped, and she had the awful feeling that Scotty was the same. Even Patrick was going out with him tonight, to the pub to watch the football. It was as if Ben had become the sun and they were all revolving around him. Especially her. She'd dropped everything to become his satellite and couldn't for the life of her think of a way to break free of his orbit. Quite frankly, she was terrified.

She was brought back to the moment by the sound of chairs scraping and nodded pleasantly at the departing parents in front of her. Two of them, obviously, wearing wedding rings and holding hands. In their early thirties. The way parents should be. Not like her, a messed-up scrap of a girl with a head like blancmange. Poor Scotty had definitely drawn the short straw there.

She walked over to Mrs Pollock, settled herself in the midget chair. Put on her professional kind-of-mother face as the teacher pulled Scotty's books from a massive cardboard box.

"Hello, Miss Harte," she said, smiling. She was lovely, Mrs Pollock. A woman in her fifties with the world's biggest bosom. Seriously, it was enormous, and looked so comfortable even Pippa had the urge to rest her head on it and cry. She knew Scotty did, and occasionally wondered if he'd develop some kind of nanny-fetish when he was older.

"Scotty is doing really well, overall," she said. "His reading is coming on and his numeracy is very promising. He's still on the shy side, but over the last few weeks I've noticed a real difference in him. He's started to really come out of his shell. Do you mind me asking if there have been any changes at home?"

"Um...no, not really," said Pippa. Unless you counted the arrival of Prince Charming, and the fact that his big sister was busy getting bonked all over the place every night. Please Lord, she thought, don't let him know about that...and even more please, don't let him have mentioned it to his teacher. It brought a whole new meaning to the word "inappropriate".

"It's just that he's drawn this. We asked them to do pictures of the best thing they could hope for – we had all kinds of things, as you can imagine," said Mrs Pollock, "a lot of games consols and bouncy castles and puppies and princess carriages. Scotty's was a bit different, though. You'll see what I mean."

She opened up the exercise book and spread the pages wide, holding them down with her fingers so Pippa could see them on the other side of the desk.

She peered down. It was a pencil drawing of a family. A stick woman with lashings of yellow hair, with the scrawled letters Pip underneath. The twins, who for some reason both had eyes bigger than their bodies. Patrick, with a bright-red face and boots so big they looked like clown feet. Scotty himself, holding what appeared to be the Olympic torch but which was probably meant to be an ice- cream cone. And a man standing in the middle of it all, taller than everyone else, so out of proportion he looked like a giant. With a scribble of black hair and a huge, upturned smile. Beneath it, in his just-forming letters, with the "a" back to front, Scotty had written one word.

Dad.

Chapter 10

When she woke up the next morning, Pippa immediately realised something was very wrong. She was alone.

Feeling a flood of panic, she glanced at the alarm clock on her bedside cabinet. 8am. At least two hours past her usual Scotty wake-up call, and still no sign of him.

She jumped out of bed, dragged on a dressing gown and ran along the hallway to his room. Flinging open the door, she saw his messy, slept-in bed, the gaggle of soft toys and action figures he cuddled up with every night scattered across the room. His pyjamas, in a huddle on the floor, next to his little slippers. But no Scotty.

Pippa trotted down the stairs, stubbing her toe painfully as she went, and followed the sound of voices to the living room.

She breathed a hefty sigh of relief as she saw Scotty sitting next to the twins on the sofa, laughing at the cartoons on the television. All three of them were dressed in their school uniform and had bowls of cereal resting on their laps. They slurped and chewed in unison, so distracted by Kung Fu Panda they barely noticed her.

Patrick was standing behind the couch, staring in confusion at the pile of bobbles and hair slides he held in his hand, hitting himself repeatedly on the head with the hairbrush like a mental patient.

"Sis, thank God!" he said, looking up as she entered the room. "Daisy and Lily say they want bunches – what the hell are bunches?

And how do you use all this elastic stuff? I haven't got a clue and they've threatened to call Childline unless I get it right...how do you *do* all this every day? I told them to eat their breakfast in the kitchen and they just ignored me and put the bloody telly on! All of them have lost a shoe and the twins say they need £1.50 each for a smoothie at lunchtime – I think they're swindling me...we've only been up an hour and I'm knackered! Was I like this?"

Pippa smiled, feeling her body relax now she knew everyone was safe, well and apparently surviving without her.

"Believe me, Patrick, you were much worse! I seem to remember one morning Mum found you eating your Weetabix in the pigsty..."

She walked over, took the bobbles from his hand and started to drag the brush through Daisy's hair. Without pausing from eating her breakfast, she immediately started to yell "ouch!" at the top of her voice as Pippa detangled her wild blonde tresses.

"Oh stop moaning," she said, trying to be as gentle as she could. "Do you think Rapunzel complains every morning when she gets her hair brushed?"

"No," murmured Scotty. "Rapunzel is perfect. Daisy's just a big fat cry-baby."

Pippa ignored the ensuing verbal battle and managed to get both the girls' hair into passably neat ponytails. There were milk stains on Scotty's shirt, but apart from that everyone was decent enough to pass muster at the school gate. And at least they'd eaten something other than chocolate – which she'd have put good money on Patrick giving them for breakfast. She was obviously under-estimating him again.

Hair crisis averted, she turned to face her brother, who was looking about a decade older than usual.

"Now, do you mind telling me what's going on? Why are they up with you? Why are you up at all? Have you done something terrible you're scared of telling me about? You haven't got someone pregnant, have you?"

"Ha! You're one to talk! And no, I've done nothing, for a change. So get off your high horse – we just thought you'd enjoy a rest. And the chance to get ready."

She narrowed her eyes at him, preparing for battle. She wasn't quite sure she trusted the new, improved Patrick just yet. Years of mischief couldn't be wiped away by a few weeks of good behaviour. There was too much water under that particular bridge for her to forget everything because of one little sleep-in.

"Who is 'we'?" she said. "And get ready for what? Do I have an appointment with PC Winnerley today?"

"Oh, give me a break – I haven't done anything, honest! 'We' is me and Ben. We went the pub last night, didn't we, to watch that crap match? Met Mr Jensen there, though, had a bit of a laugh. Got the phone number of that new barmaid. Reckon I'm well in there. Anyway, Ben thought you might want a bit of a rest. Personally I think you're a bit of a layabout, but the old geezers were of the opinion you work too hard. So tonight, you're going away. With Ben. And Mr Jensen's coming over here and we're looking after the kids."

"I am not! And you are not!" she said, outraged at the thought of the three of them plotting behind her back. At the thought of Ben discussing her at all. At all of it. It was wrong, and it was out of control, and she had a headache, and the toe she'd stubbed was throbbing, and she thought she might cry.

After her outburst on the hill and Scotty's fantasy family drawing, the last thing she wanted to feel was ganged-up on. And even more out of control.

"Yeah, you are. I know I'm a bit of a liability, but Mr Jensen's raised five kids. It's not like he doesn't know what he's doing. And you keep going on about me growing up and taking a bit of responsibility – how am I ever going to do that if you keep treating me like the village idiot, sis? You're going away. A night of Scrabble with Ben. Get some of the triple-letter words, like, maybe that one that starts with 's' and ends with 'x'..."

She thumped him, hard, with the back of the hairbrush, realising that she was laughing. She didn't want to laugh. She wanted to be angry. To be upset. To stay in the saddle, firmly perched on her high horse, thank you very much.

But he was funny, Patrick. She'd forgotten how funny he could be. She'd forgotten how good he could be to be around. Some sister she was. He was also right...he'd never learn, never get a chance to prove himself, if she never gave him the opportunity to try. Had she become so trapped in her own martyred world of self-sacrifice that she'd held him back? Had she turned him bad by being too good? Ouch! The thought made her brain hurt, but she had to acknowledge the possibility. And maybe – just maybe – give him the chance he said he needed. He'd done this, for her – no matter how hard he was trying to sound flippant, he'd organised it. So she could relax. It wasn't his fault that Ben was causing her more of a headache than a heart flip at the moment.

She couldn't say no, she knew. Even though she'd probably regret it. She'd probably come home and find the twins drinking cider straight from the barrel, and Scotty riding SpongeBob around Bottom Paddock in his Spiderman costume. At the very least she'd come home to a load of empty pizza boxes and an almighty mess to clear up.

That, though, she could handle. She'd been tidying up their mess for years. It was the rest she wasn't sure about. A whole night with Ben. A whole night with the man she'd called a perfect moron the day before. A whole night to talk and laugh, and enjoy that Scrabble word Patrick had mentioned. A whole night to fall even deeper into the hole she felt herself slipping into.

Because while parents' night had shown her how much the kids loved having him in their lives, it had also reminded her of how much she felt the same.

She looked at the kids. At the telly. At Patrick. And desperately wanted a way out. An excuse to run, to hide. To start the day over and do it different. To start her entire life over and do it different.

"You're going," he said firmly, "so don't even try. No excuses. I even know what bunches are now."

By midday she was still packing. Asking Patrick what she should take had earned her the kind of look she'd probably given him hundreds of times in recent years: the one that said, "what do you expect me to do about it?" The one that said, frankly, "grow a pair and sort yourself out".

Verbally, he'd replied: "I don't know. I've only just mastered bunches, sis, don't ask me to pack for a mini-break as well. I'm not bloody Bridget Jones, am I? If it was me, it'd be a large jar of Nutella and a multi-pack of condoms."

She'd shivered at the thought of him combining the two and distracted herself from her anxieties by shoving pretty much every item of clothing she owned into a rucksack. A rucksack that was still only half-full, despite containing all of her wardrobe. Several pairs of holey jeans. Vest tops. Fleeces. Mismatched socks. And the one "proper" dress she had – short, tight, black. It had been way too grown up for her when she'd bought it, her little teenaged brain filled with the images of Oxford balls and handsome strangers, and she suspected it was still way too grown up for her now. Especially as the only tights she had were still held together with nail varnish. Sometimes, she thought, being a girl just sucked. Especially when you were this bad at it.

She heard the sound of a vehicle pull up outside and deduced that Ben had arrived. Brilliant. A whole morning to prepare and she still wasn't ready. It felt like weeks since she'd seen him, even though it was only hours.

She shoved a hairbrush and some lip gloss into the bag and trotted down the stairs with as much enthusiasm as she could muster. Her feet weren't capable of moving very fast – all of her energy seemed to have been diverted into her heart, which was beating so fast she felt as if she'd drunk eight cups of coffee. Which, now she thought about it, she probably had. She was scared, wired and jittery – perfect date material. Any man would be delighted.

Pippa pulled on her jacket – the old velvet one her mum had always called "vintage" – and twisted her face into something resembling a smile. Time to man up. She might feel like hell, but Patrick, Mr Jensen and yes, even Ben, had gone to a heck of a lot of trouble to organise this for her. It would be just plain ungrateful to walk out there looking like a French aristocrat on her way to the guillotine.

She paused to glance around the farmhouse kitchen. Dirty dishes in the sink. Toast crumbs on the pine table. Cracks in the floor tiles. Scotty's collection of precious found objects cluttering up the mantelpiece. It was a mess, but it was her mess. Theirs. It was home, and it was love, and it was safety. And she felt something approaching a sense of tragedy about leaving it – some portent of doom so strong she half expected a crow to come flying through the open window and crash beak-first into the Aga.

She was gripped with an agonising need to see the kids. To cuddle Scotty and kiss Daisy and Lily. To hold them tight and comfort them the way she always had...God, she wished they weren't at school.

For the first time, she realised that the comfort went both ways – that she needed them as much as they needed her. That they'd looked after her as much as she'd looked after them. Because, really, without them, what would have happened to her after her parents died? Would she be backpacking around Asia, or would she simply have curled up in a ball of pain and faded into the west, with no reason to carry on? All this time, she thought she'd been making them secure – when a lot of it was the other way around. Now she was stripped bare of all her defences. No kids. No chores. No pressing need to be dodging cowpats in the paddock. She should have been thrilled – but instead she felt exposed, vulnerable. Like a skinny-twigged tree blown naked by autumn winds.

She shook it off, told herself she was being a dumb ass and unlatched the door. She'd be back in a matter of hours – and it would all still be there waiting for her. Especially the dishes.

Outside, she found Mr Jensen and Patrick standing next to each other, working their way through an open packet of custard creams. She could see some chocolate digestives and several tubes of Pringles peeking out of the carrier bag at their feet. Ah. A balanced dinner for the children.

They were both grinning up at Ben, who was waving at them from the cab of the van. The very old, very battered VW camper that he appeared to be driving. It was painted in three colours – red, cream and rust – an old-fashioned "splitty". Exactly the kind that her dad used to drive them around in. Different colours, yes, and minus the CND stickers in the windows, but essentially the same.

Pippa felt her heart squeeze out an extra couple of beats. She'd told him about it and he'd remembered. He'd remembered and he'd found one, and it was all for her, and that was so sweet, and really, she thought she might cry. Again. And if she started, she'd never stop. She'd carry on crying until she flooded Bottom Paddock and had to be rushed into hospital with dehydration, or the whole village was swept away on a tidal wave of the emotion she'd been keeping clenched inside her.

She squeezed her eyelids so tight the tears were forced back in, as Patrick ambled over to her.

"Brilliant, isn't it?" he said, nudging her so hard she almost fell over. She nodded, not trusting herself to speak.

Patrick saw the expression on her face and pulled her into a hug. A huge, big-brother hug that made her wonder if he was part bear. While he had her trapped, he whispered into her ear, "You know what you always say to me, Pip?"

"No, what?" she replied, expecting the worst.

"Don't be such a knob."

"I never say that to you, Patrick!"

"Okay, but I know you're thinking it – and it applies here. To you. Me and Mr Jensen have got it all under control. Ben's dead excited and you should be too. Go off, enjoy yourself. It's a camper van, not a torture wagon. Scoot – and make sure you don't tell me all about it when you get back."

He gave her a light shove in the small of her back and she hopped, skipped and jumped her way to the open van door. Ben smiled down at her. He was wearing Levis again and a t-shirt tight enough to show off the awesome shoulders. His hair was slightly too long, giving him a wild, edgy look. Like a pirate who'd come to kidnap her. But his eyes...his eyes were gentle. Soft. Slightly concerned. As stunts went, this one was a risky one – would she love the fact he'd tried to recreate a happy family memory or would she burst into tears and run shrieking back into the cocoon of the farmhouse?

"Miss Harte," he said, keeping the tone as light as he could, "your chariot awaits."

Chapter 11

They headed, as she'd known they would, to Barrelstock Bay. It was different in the daylight – still quiet, but not deserted. A few dog-walkers and ramblers dotted the beach and the cliff pathways; a lone ice-cream van doing solitary business in the almost-empty carpark.

They walked and they should have talked. But something inside Pippa was still wound so tight she couldn't let it out. Something was coiled in her tummy, strangling her emotions, deadening the pleasure she knew she should be feeling. She kept wondering what time it was, whether Patrick would remember to pick the kids up from school, whether he'd crash the jeep on the way home. Whether they'd eat anything but custard creams and crisps for tea. Whether he'd get drunk and leave them all alone while he visited that new barmaid he had his eye on.

She knew that wasn't what she was really worried about. She knew she was using all of that as some form of defence, that her crippled brain was trying to distract her from the real problem: the tall, handsome man walking beside her, holding her hand firmly in his.

"I'm sorry, Pippa," he said, after a few minutes of silence.

For what, she wondered? For existing? For messing up my perfectly ordered life? For making me feel alive for the first time in years? For making me realise that I do have needs, after all, and giving me the sneaking suspicion that you are the only man who can meet them?

"Why?" she asked, with a voice so small he barely heard it over the crash of the waves.

"I'm sorry about the camper van, about coming here. I thought you'd like it, that it would remind you of happy times, but I can see...it doesn't. It was insensitive of me and I'm sorry."

She stopped and he stood still beside her. It was a bright, cool day, dazzling sunshine and jumper-wearing temperatures. Rays of sun dappled over his hair, bringing out shades she'd never noticed before: golds and auburns and glints of chestnut. She reached up, wound her fingers into its thick, dark waves. He nuzzled into her hand, kissing her palm so softly, so sweetly, but with such promise that it made her clench and tighten lower down.

"You have nothing to be sorry about," she said, looking up at him with the full force of those cornflower-blue eyes. "It was a lovely thing to think of and it hasn't upset me. This...mood...is nothing to do with you."

That wasn't strictly speaking true, but it would be just plain rude to blame him for the fact that she was having a fit of the collywobbles.

He pulled her close to him, and her face fell against the firm plain of his chest. She automatically inhaled his scent: wood, spice, sex on a stick. Her arms wound their way around his waist and she felt herself start to deflate slowly, from the inside out. As though she was a giant balloon and someone had just popped her.

Ben stroked her hair, kissed the top of her head, held her so tight and so long that she thought she might melt. When he finally let her go, when she could finally breathe again, she felt different. Better. Happier. As if the physical contact alone had somehow chased away the black dog; as if one super-hug from Ben Retallick had rendered her so senseless that all of her creeping fears and sneaky little doubts had run screaming, locking themselves away in the cupboards where she usually kept them.

And that, alone, was enough to tell her she was right to be scared. When she felt bad, Ben fixed it. When she felt weak, Ben gave her strength. When she felt worried, Ben made her smile. And when she felt horny...well, Ben sorted that out as well. He was a rock and she was a stream flowing around him. He had become part of her world, as important to her as the air she breathed.

She loved him. And he was going to leave her.

"You look amazing," said Ben, as she walked into the bar. She'd thought Barrelstock Bay was it for the night, that they'd be roughing it in the camper van, making love beneath the stars and sleeping in socks and bobble hats to stay warm. All of which would have been fine with her.

But Ben had different ideas. He'd taken the date night seriously and booked them into Tregowan Lodge – a place Pippa knew existed, but had never visited. It was, she'd been told, a "boutique hotel", and most definitely not the kind of place where locals would ever stay, for fear of being labelled soft in the head. The prices were crazy, and one night there could have paid for several new dishwashers. In the sale.

Ben had taken one look at her face as they'd pulled up into the car park and burst out laughing.

"What?" she asked, giving him a slitty-eyed look that told him to shut-the-mollusc-up, or risk losing a vital body part.

"Your face," he replied. "It's priceless. You look as if someone's forcing you to spend the night in a flea-infested crackhouse."

"Hmm. I'd probably feel more comfortable there. Have you any idea how much it costs to stay here? This isn't for people like me. I live here, for goodness' sake."

"Snob," he said, jumping down from the step of the camper and grabbing their bags.

"Snob? How can you say that?" she shrieked, falling into step beside him as they walked towards the imposing colonnaded doorway. It had been a minor manor house in days gone by and she had to admit the location was amazing. Perched on the side of the cliff, almost as though it was growing out of it, with eye-dazzling views of the bay below. It was beautiful, with layers of terraced gardens creeping down the sides, tiny patios with tables and chairs sitting beside the steps to the coastal path. Presumably so you could stop and have a G&T on your way, she thought. It was so far outside her comfort zone she didn't know quite where to put herself.

"You are being an inverted snob, Pippa Harte," he said, "as well as a selfish baby. Some of us are on holiday, you know."

"Huh. Your whole life seems to be a holiday," she sniped, whispering it as they entered the lobby. It was all country-chic and fresh flowers and smiling staff and copies of *Harper's Bazaar* scattered artfully on antique side tables. It was just plain weird and made her head hurt.

She was, though, she had to admit, as he handled checking in, being a bit of a baby. He'd planned this. He'd done it to please her. The least she could do was try and enjoy it and stop being such a girl freak.

She kept reminding herself of that as she holed up in an en-suite bathroom that was the size of her lounge. Ben was getting ready in the bedroom and said he'd see her downstairs. She pulled the little black dress out and stared at it critically as she hung it up over the shower rail. Maybe the steam would help with the creases and the ladder in those tights was right at the very top. Any man who got that far was probably not in the mood to be critical anyway.

After almost an hour of, as Patrick would put it "fannying about" she decided she was as glamorous as she was going to get. She was clean, her hair was shiny and straight and she smelled fantastic – those hotel toiletries were definitely going in her bag before they left. There was a hint of clear lip gloss, mascara, and yes, a real-life, very grown-up frock, together with ancient black stilettos that were nowhere as easy to walk in as wellies.

In fact, she didn't look, smell or feel anything at all like her usual self. And maybe that, she thought, giving her hair a final poof in the mirror, isn't at all a bad thing. She'd been feeling shaky all day; suffering from some kind of minor emotional seizure as a result of finally being honest with herself. Finally admitting in her own screwed-up brain that she didn't just fancy Ben Retallick. She didn't just like his biceps, or his bottom or his bedroom skills. She loved him and it was too late to stop it. It was like standing in front of a car going at 100mph on the motorway: you knew you should be throwing yourself out of the way, but for some reason your feet were stuck. Like in one of those anxiety dreams where all the door handles fall off the minute you touch them.

None of that, she decided, was Ben's fault. He couldn't help being totally awesome in every way, any more than he could help being too damaged to make this stick. It was like the ladder in her tights. It was there and she knew it was there, but if she was very careful and distracted him just enough, maybe he wouldn't notice.

The way he looked at her as she walked into the hotel bar, though...she wasn't quite sure. His dark eyes drank her in, seemed to devour every inch of her. She saw his pupils dilate and was suddenly full of the thrill of being a woman. The girl stuff had seemed to be such a chore, so irrelevant to her life and now it filled her up. Made her feel powerful and strong and kind of squishy in her nether regions. That look alone, that one very male, very assessing, look was enough to make her forget potential heartache and pain, and just feel wanted. For now, she thought, that would have to be enough.

"You look more than amazing. You look like an angel," he said, "one who needs to be thoroughly defiled."

He stood up to kiss her. She put a bit of heat into it, brushing his tongue with hers in a way she knew she shouldn't do in public, and was rewarded with a quiet growl that seemed to come from somewhere deep inside him.

"Be careful," he said, "or we won't be making it to dinner."

She let her hands roam over his body, skimming his backside in its tailored suit trousers, melting herself into him like running water.

"Maybe I don't want dinner," she whispered back, feeling him stiffen in response. Lord. Being in love seemed to be making her reckless, she thought. Maybe it was the realisation that she had nothing else to lose – it was already gone.

Ben kissed her neck until her knees turned to rubber and she half collapsed into his arms, earning them a few looks from staff and other guests.

"They're just jealous," he said, but pulled away. He held her hand, steadying her, and walked her into the dining room. Pippa felt her eyes pop at the decor, all subtle golds and bronzes, table linen so white it glowed in the candlelight.

"Feeling all right?" he asked, sitting across from her at their table for two. "You seemed a bit...wobbly back there."

"It was just the high heels," she replied, "nothing to do with you at all. You don't move me in the slightest."

He smiled, an edge of arrogance showing her just how little he believed that last statement. Which was fair enough as it was a load of old codswallop.

"If this was a film," she said, looking at the menu, "I'd let you order for me."

"Do you want me to?" he asked, quirking an eyebrow upwards.

"Yes," she replied, "but only because I don't know how to pronounce most of the stuff on here. I'm just a country bumpkin, see?"

"Yeah, right," he said, laughter dancing in the chocolate of his eyes. "And I'm Luke Skywalker. You should have been an Oxford graduate by now. I'm guessing there's not a thing on this menu you couldn't pronounce better than the chef, so don't give me that small-town-girl routine. You, Pippa Harte, are like no other woman I've ever met."

She grinned at him as she studied the menu, and he realised he'd meant every word of that. She wasn't like anyone else in the known universe. Today, she'd been anxious, off-balance, quiet. He'd been so worried that he'd upset her with the camper-van thing, or the talking-under-the-oak-tree thing, or any of the other things he knew he was capable of doing to upset a woman. And yet, here she was, looking like all his fantasies come true, laughing and joking and, yes, touching him up with her shoeless toes under the table. Her stockinged foot edged its way up his thigh, heading for the obvious destination, and he almost cringed as he felt the inevitable male reaction take hold.

"What are you doing?" he asked. "I'm going to knock the table over if you carry on like that."

"Helping you feel the Force," she replied, looking at him impishly over the leather-bound menu.

"Believe me, I can feel it," he said, closing his eyes for a second to try and bring himself back under control. "Now stop that, so I can concentrate, and we can have a conversation, like two grown-up people out on a date."

"Grown up. Hah! That'll be the day," she said, looking around the room. "I feel like an under-age drinker in this place. Everyone else is old enough to be my dad."

He scanned the room and realised she was right. They were easily the youngest people there. Everyone else was senior: some in their fifties, some much older. All seemed to be in couples, locked in their own realities, their own conversations, their own worlds. Worlds they'd probably shared for decades. He thought it was very romantic, which possibly meant he'd turned into some kind of super-sap. The Pippa effect.

They ordered their food – Pippa pronouncing everything perfectly – and he poured them both some red wine.

"I came here with my granddad that summer," he said, after a few sips.

"The summer of Oak Tree Gate?" she asked.

"The very same. It had just opened up as a restaurant, and he came to have what he called a 'bit of a nosy'. Nobody from his generation thought it would survive. The old-school farmers, they didn't see the potential of this kind of tourism."

"The kind where people assume, because they're re-mortgaging their homes to stay here for the night, that it must be something utterly fantastic, and tell all their friends they simply must come as well?"

"Exactly. He thought it was a load of nonsense. But now he's gone and this place is still here."

Pippa laid a hand over his on the table. It was clenched into a fist and she knew that meant he was tense, that something unwanted and dark had skittered over his brain like an evil spider.

"What happened with him?" she asked, "I know you miss him."

He twined his fingers into hers, met her gaze. Knew he could tell her things he had never been able to tell another human being.

"He committed suicide," he said. "When the banks foreclosed, he killed himself. Did it the old-fashioned farmer's way, shotgun to the head. Couldn't face up to life after he'd lost everything. His wife had died years before; my parents were – still are – living in Australia. Apart from the farm, I was all he had left. And I was busy, in London, living my successful and glamorous life. He was too proud to tell me what was going on and I was too busy to ask. There was work, Johanna, all the distractions that I thought back then were important. I didn't make time for him, and then it was too late. He was gone. Didn't want to be a burden to anyone."

He finally looked up. He'd been staring at the table as he spoke, as though that was the only way he'd be able to get the words out. He looked up into Pippa's perfect face to see tears falling from her eyes. She pulled his hand towards her and kissed it, gently, putting all the love she could into that one small gesture.

"It wasn't your fault," she said. "You know that, Ben Retallick. You're too intelligent not to know it."

"Knowing it and feeling it are too different things, Pippa Harte. But thank you. It feels...it feels good to finally talk about it. To let some of it out."

He blew out a harsh, tense breath, and his slightly-too-long fringe lifted on his forehead. He squeezed her fingers, as though he was the one reassuring her, not the other way around.

"Better stop now, though," he said, trying for light and failing, "if I carry on sharing like this, I'll end up on the Jerry Springer Show or something."

"Don't," she said, shaking her head so her hair shimmered around her shoulders, gold pouring over the black of her dress. "Don't make light. This isn't light. It's very, very dark. It's so painful to lose someone you love, but to live with guilt about it is even worse. And I understand why things happened the way they did now."

"What things?" he asked.

"McConnell. The way you attacked him. I've known you for a while now and everything I've seen of you goes against the idea of you simply cracking, losing your temper like that. You're not made like that, Ben. You're too controlled. But him coming to you afterwards, laughing about that old man who killed himself – it must have brought it all back. It must have reminded you of your granddad. That's what happened, isn't it?"

He nodded, gazing at her wordlessly. She was so very, very special. She got it. She understood. Johanna had known about his grandfather, but if she'd ever made the connection between the two events, it hadn't had any bearing on her reaction to his conviction.

For the millionth time since meeting Pippa again, he wondered how he had ever allowed himself to fall for a woman like Johanna. Had she been different once? Or had he been so very different then that he hadn't noticed her flaws? Comparing her to Pippa was like comparing candlelight to the blazing sun; a trickling stream to the Atlantic Ocean. He'd felt attracted to Johanna in a way he thought was passionate, until Pippa. He'd enjoyed spending time with her in a way he thought was solid and companionable, until Pippa. What he felt for Johanna had been nothing compared to what this old-soul-in-a-gorgeous-young-body across the table brought out in him.

And still, when Johanna had left him, he'd felt devastated. How would he feel if he lost Pippa? It was too terrifying to contemplate.

"Come on," she said, standing up so fast she tottered in her heels.

"Come on where?" he asked, confused, anxious and pleased all at once – because right then he so didn't want to be in a room full of over-stuffed people sitting in over-stuffed chairs.

"We're going out for some air. Don't argue."

"As if I'd dare," he replied, following her as she left the room. She collared a waiter on the way, told them to hold their food for them and strutted – yes, definitely strutted, he thought, as he watched her rear view – out through the French windows and onto the terrace.

The evening was cool, but not goosebump-cold, and the night sky glittered with the vivid blanket of stars you only ever see miles away from the city. She left the door open and old-style band music wafted out towards them. The tune had a gentle swing, like the background to something black and white and glamorous with Fred and Ginger in it.

She fell into his arms and he automatically held her there, burying his face in the yellow cloud of her hair. It smelled different, but with her constant underlying scent of lavender. The scent he would forever associate with her and these golden days in Cornwall.

"I can't dance at all," she said into his chest. "But I've watched a lot of those dancing shows on telly, and you're probably old enough to have had ballroom lessons as a kid."

He snorted with laughter, managing a smile when he thought he'd truly run out of them.

"Of course. Accompanied by madrigals and harpsichords, naturally. Just follow my lead..."

He lifted her hand into his, taking her into a classic waltz pose, but with way too much body contact for it to have been done in public. She glued herself to him, only her shoulders leaning back, so they could look at each other in the silvery paint of the moonlight.

Slowly, they moved around the terrace, quiet, lost in the music, in the moonlight, and each other's eyes. Giving comfort without words, taking solace in the silence and offering each other an unspoken sip of their souls.

Pippa looked up at him, at the tiny creases around his eyes, the wide line of his mouth, the way his hair curled slightly onto the collar of his white shirt. Felt his hips pressed against hers, felt all the power and strength in those arms honed down to the gentle touch of his fingers wrapped around hers as they glided in time to the beat.

She leaned up, kissed him softly and briefly, felt his body flare into immediate response.

"Dinner in the room?" he said, making it a question.

"Perfect," she replied.

Chapter 12

Pippa hoisted two melons up in front of her chest, one in each hand and pulled an "oo-er missus" face.

"What do you think?" she said, wiggling them at Ben like a fruity fake cleavage.

"I think that's a lovely pair, but I'm more than happy with what nature gave you," he replied, his mouth curved up into a lopsided grin.

"Bloody good job as well," she said, carefully placing the produce back into its place on the exotic fruit display.

"Why?" he asked, knowing he was stepping into a carefully laid Pippa-trap and not really caring.

"Because if you'd thought otherwise, I'd be taking you off to the prize marrow stand for a fitting..."

"Ouch," he said, pulling her into him for a kiss. "Hit a man where his ego is, eh? And what are melons doing at a Summer Fayre in Cornwall anyway?"

"It's the Eden effect. Everyone wants to show off their greenhouse skills these days. I secretly suspect they buy them from Sainsbury's the night before, but it's more than my life's worth to say anything. Are you enjoying yourself?"

As she asked, she gave his groin a little bump and grind, wiggling her skinny-jean-clad hips against him.

"Yes," he said, closing his eyes and enjoying the moment. "My marrow is extremely pleased with the whole situation. What about you?"

"I'm having a wonderful time, thank you very much. I don't want to bring you and your marrow down, but it means a lot to me that you stayed for today. It can get tough, for me, for Patrick and having you around is...well, distracting. Even if you do have to leave later."

Two weeks had passed since their trip to Tregowan Lodge. Two weeks since they'd woken up together for the first ever time, tangled in million-thread-count sheets, fuzzy from drinking champagne in bed, fuzzy from too much sex and, in Pippa's case, fuzzy from all the pieces that had fallen into place the day before.

She'd come back to consciousness a few minutes before him – her body clock was set to stupid o'clock wherever she was, thanks to Scotty. And she'd used those minutes wisely, enjoying the freedom to watch him, to study his face as he slept. To gently trace the curve of his lips, brush his hair from his eyes. To give in to all of the emotion she felt flooding through her: all of the love.

She'd never tell him she was in love with him, she'd decided. It wasn't fair. They'd struck a deal. They'd had The Talk. He'd made it clear that while his marrow was fond of her melons, more than that wasn't on the cards. It was a match made in greengrocer heaven, but nothing more.

Of course, she'd been a prize idiot to think she could ever settle so lightly for anything that casual. Years of solitude, years of coping alone, completely destroyed by one admittedly pretty fantastic man. And yet...as he slept there, the muscle of his chest rising and falling, sheets tugged askew to reveal the strong lines of his thigh, she couldn't find it in herself to regret anything. If this was love, she'd take it. Any way she could, for as long as it lasted.

Most people, she suspected, never experienced this in their entire lifetimes. And even if it would eventually come at a huge price – for her and for everyone around her – for the time being, she wanted to enjoy it. Savour it. Memorise it.

She'd slipped her hand beneath the covers, traced her fingertips up the inside of his thigh, waited for him to respond in the way she knew he would. His eyes had snapped open and his lips curled into a lazily lustful smile.

He lifted the sheets, looked down at himself and did a comedic pretend double-take.

"Damn," he said, pulling her down to crash against him, "where did that come from? See what you do to me? Even when I'm asleep?"

She did know. And she intended to remind him, over and over again, as often as she could.

Now, two weeks on, she was facing up to the fact that he was leaving – however temporarily. He'd broken the news to her a few nights before and she got the distinct impression that he should actually have gone ages ago. That she wasn't the only one neglecting the duties of "real life".

His book was due to come out in less than two months' time and instead of meeting with his publishers he'd been ravishing her in deepest, darkest Cornwall. As distracted as they both were, time had started to take on a life of its own – a life that revolved around the kids going to school, Pippa getting her chores done and the two of them grabbing as much time together as they could.

She'd taken her fear, her insecurity and buried it in a deep dark place – not wanting to waste any of her precious time with him. As a result she'd felt liberated, wild, reckless – and Ben had a look of constant surprise on his face. He wasn't complaining – really, even she knew, what man would? But they'd both known it couldn't stay like that. They were burning bright, like a supernova about to implode.

The fact that he'd been intending to leave on that particular day had made it harder – it was the annual village show and she wanted him there – for all kinds of reasons.

"I need to be in London for a meeting on Monday morning," he'd said, twining his fingers into her hair as they lay snuggled up together in the bedroom of Honeysuckle Cottage. Outside, she could hear Harry Potter squealing frantic oinks, and Phineas and Ferb hissing back at him. Trouble in farmyard paradise.

"But..." he'd added, "it'll only take a couple of days. There's stuff I need to do, people I need to talk to. Publicity things to arrange. And then...then I'll come back. If you want me to."

"Of course I do...but it's a shame you'll miss the show," she'd replied, trying to staunch the panic that was spreading across her heart like cracks on an ice-coated pond. Get a grip of yourself, woman, she thought. Think about something else. Think about pigs in war paint and cammo. Think geese with rocket launchers. Think farm-a-geddon; think anything but him leaving.

"Why?" he asked, sensing from her tone of voice that there was more to it than cream teas and pinning rosettes on prize-winning dairy cows.

"Well, it's the highlight of the social calendar around here..." she'd said.

"Funnily enough, having lived here for the last few months, I do believe that," he replied, kissing her gently on the lips, "but why else? You sound...weird."

"Weirder than usual?"

"Yes, and stop stalling – what is it?"

"Okay. Sorry to be weird. But... it's also the day we think of as the anniversary of our parents' death. It was on their way back from a neighbour's house after the show that the crash happened. And every year Patrick marks the occasion by doing something joyous like stealing a tractor or punching the vicar in the cassocks. Which actually has its merits...it always keeps me distracted, anyway, and stops me feeling too sorry for myself. "

Ben was silent, wrapping his arms tightly around her, throwing one long leg across the line of her hips until she was completely enveloped in the velvet muscle of his body. God, it felt good.

"Well I think I'd better stay, then, at least for some of it. I'll drive back to London in the afternoon," he said. "I think Patrick might just behave himself this year, so you'll need someone else to distract you instead, which happens to be one of my specialist subjects. Anyway, I'm hoping there's a Miss Knobbly Knees contest. I'm going to sign you up for it."

"I do not have knobbly knees!" Pippa shrieked, trying to slap him, but finding her arms trapped at her sides.

"You haven't seen them from the angles I have..." he'd replied, sliding further down the bed to demonstrate.

He'd been as good as his word and found all kinds of inventive ways to distract her over the next few days. So successfully that she was actually enjoying herself at the show for the first time in years, strolling around the stalls with him, poking gentle fun at the even gentler rhythms of country life.

The day had dawned blissfully sunny and the kids were running around in shorts and jam-stained t-shirts, spending the pocket money they'd been given, occasionally darting back to them to show off the wonderful items they'd won on the tombola and the Splat the Rat stand. Scotty was especially proud of the bottle of Brut aftershave he'd scooped, insisting that Ben wear it there and then.

"Oooh," said Pippa, sniffing his neck, "I am finding that disturbingly sexy...what's wrong with me?"

"Don't blame yourself," he'd replied, looking smug, "you're only flesh and blood...and now, I'm feeling so macho, I'm going to take part in the tug of war. I expect you to stand at the side and cheer for me – and possibly flash your boobs to put the other side off."

"Won't that put you off as well?" she asked, smiling innocently.

"No. I'm a man of steel when it comes to these things," he lied.

He'd ended up on a team with Patrick, his friend Robbie and, as was the way of these things, the head mistress of the local primary school.

As Pippa stood and watched, Scotty, Lily and Daisy screaming themselves hoarse beside her, she realised she'd never felt so happy, even on this most unlikely of days. It was the anniversary of losing her parents, Ben was leaving later and the day after held the unparalleled joy of her quarterly Social Services review. But somehow, right then, right there, none of that mattered. Everything just felt... perfect – and if the world froze in that one moment she'd have had the best that life could throw at a human being.

The kids were happy and healthy, Patrick was growing up and there was a man in her life who had finally shown her what love was all about. What living was all about.

The man in question was stripped down to his jeans, the bulk of his bare chest sweating with the strain as he heaved and pulled. His skin was tanned and smooth, biceps curling and swelling as he leaned back and tugged, heels dug in and face contorted with the effort.

Eventually the other side yielded and everyone fell in a big heap on the grass. Patrick reached out and offered his hand and Ben jumped effortlessly to his feet, face split with the mindless grin that all men seem to get when they win something stupid and sporty.

He walked towards her and she wiped a clump of grass and dirt from his flat stomach, her fingers trailing over the outline of his rather stupendous almost-six-pack, her mind already taking up residence in the gutter as she explored the hard ridges of his flesh. God, she thought, was definitely a woman – who else could have invented something as spectacular as this?

"Like what you see, Miss Harte?" he asked, raising her face up to his for a kiss. He smelled of fresh sweat and grass and sunshine. With a hint of 1970s aftershave thrown in. It was altogether too lush.

"Not really, but you're the best I have to hand..." she replied, giving his backside a quick squeeze. "You're going to stink on your way back to London. Glad I won't be trapped in a car with you."

"They do actually have showers in London, you know," he said. "Talking of which..."

Pippa buried her head in his chest, screwing up her eyes against tears she knew were hiding there, lying in wait for a moment of girl weakness. She took a final inhale, sniffing in the scent of him, of this gentle giant she loved so very much, then looked up at him.

"I know. You need to go. Come on, I'll walk you to the car," she said.

They strolled, hand in hand, to the field that was doubling as a car park. He'd already explained to the kids that he was leaving, but that he'd be back. There had been a huge wave of protest and a distinct quivering of Scotty's lower lip, but he'd averted disaster the way adults have done for centuries: by promising to bring them presents when he returned.

He pulled his t-shirt back over his head and clicked his car door open. He leaned back against it, hair shining in the sun, eyes squinting slightly against the glare as he looked down at her. She looked so beautiful, even with her hair tied up like a messy horse's mane, wearing that old Simpsons t-shirt she loved so much. Beautiful and delicate and ever-so-slightly scared. Damn. That wasn't what he'd been aiming for at all. So much for distracting her on this crappy day.

"So," he said, reaching out to stroke a stray lock of blonde hair from her eyes, "how was it for you today?"

"Um...fine," she said. "Scarily fine, actually. So fine I may well feel a bit guilty about it later, when the happy's worn off."

He made a "humph" kind of sound and took her face between his hands, holding it gently as their eyes locked.

"Do you think that's what they would have wanted, your parents? For you to feel guilty about enjoying yourself, after everything you've done? Because I don't. I think they'd be proud of you. I know they would. You've done everything right, Pippa. You've made a terrible situation work, for you, for Patrick, for the kids. Nobody could have asked more from you. You deserve everything the world has to offer, never mind one day of fun at the village show."

She screwed her face up, really tight, and he realised she was trying to stop herself from crying. Yay. Way to go, Ben Retallick, he thought – every line a winning line. Kiss the girl and make her cry.

"Thank you," she said, finally opening her shiny eyes again. She'd won the battle, but only just.

He took her in his arms and kissed her, extremely thoroughly, until her knees started to buckle and her lungs cried out for air.

"I'll be back in a few days," he said. "That one will have to keep you going till then."

She hugged him, then pulled back and studied his face, storing up every line, every contour, every subtle shade. Locking them away in the memory bank. Just in case.

"Okay," she said, voice small, battered with too much emotion. Losing her parents. Losing Ben, for no matter how short a time, when she'd only just found him. Feeling so happy. Feeling so sad. Feeling everything, with way too much intensity.

He was about to drive away from her and spend hours on a motorway, with all kinds of crazy reckless drivers. Surrounded by all sorts of potential danger. Speeding down the fast lane, oblivious to how fragile life was – how one momentary distraction, one bad decision, one drunk driver, could change everything.

She'd lived through too much to trust him to fate so easily; she'd expected her mum and dad to come home that day years ago as well – but they never did. She knew she was being stupid, she knew he'd be fine, but still...what if he wasn't fine? What if something terrible happened on that long drive to the big city? What if he never made it home again as well? What if he ended up being cut from a twisted, burning wreck as well? The thought was enough to set her heart a-flutter in her chest, a small bird beating wings against its cage.

"Ben..." she said, as he stooped to get into the driver's seat, "Be careful. I...I love you, you know."

He paused half-crouched, stared at her as if someone had whacked him in the head with a maypole. He frowned, his eyes darkening and his lips working as though he was trying to talk but couldn't find any words.

The minute she said it, the minute she saw his reaction, she knew she'd made a terrible mistake. She'd broken all her own rules. Blown everything she'd worked so hard to protect. Revealed everything she's tried so hard to hide. She'd told the man who couldn't love that she loved him.

She was an idiot.

She turned, feeling those long-denied tears finally fight their way to the surface and ran in the opposite direction.

Chapter 13

The rest of the afternoon passed in a blur of hidden pain, fake smiles and children who seemed determined to test her to the very edges of her limits.

Patrick bailed, as she'd known he would, and took off to the pub with his ever-expanding bunch of close personal friends, leaving her alone with three tired, tempestuous youngsters at a time when she had so little left in the tank to deal with them.

By nine o'clock that night all three of them were wailing for various reasons and Pippa was fighting a desperate battle to not join in.

Lily had lost the Little Bo Peep ear muffs she'd won on the lucky dip, Daisy had a huge splinter in her thumb and Scotty, two hours past his usual bed time, was like a stick of dynamite attached to a burning fuse.

Pippa was sitting on the closed toilet lid balancing Daisy on her knee as she writhed and wriggled, trying to get away. She was holding her little hand tight to steady it as she wielded her eyebrow tweezers, after soaking the splint in warm water for five minutes first. She was screaming so loudly in her face that Pippa's eardrums were vibrating.

"Calm down! I'm not going to chop your hand off – I know it's sore but it's got to come out!" she said, wishing for the millionth time since she took up her job as "kind of mother" that someone had given her lessons first. Her own mum, she was sure, would have had a fantastic method of pain-free splinter removal tucked up her parental sleeve. Something quick and easy she could lift from the "big book of mummy secrets". Sadly she'd not passed on her copy and Pippa was left making up everything as she went, groping for answers in the dark as she tried to find her way through it all.

Lily was lying collapsed face down in the doorway to the bathroom, kicking the floor repeatedly with the fluffy pink toes of her princess slippers, sobbing that she loved her Little Bo Peep ear muffs more than anything in the "whole wide world". Scotty was standing behind her tearing small strips off the wallpaper with one hand and holding the other over his ear to block out all the noise. He was rocking backwards and forwards and holding his breath for so long he was going cross-eyed. Daisy ratcheted up the volume an extra few notches and promptly tried to poke Pippa in the eye with her *Frozen* toothbrush.

Welcome to my life, thought Pippa, squinting in pain as her eye watered. This is exactly what I dreamed of when I was a little girl in my own princess slippers, about a million years ago.

She finally snagged the corner of the tiny slither of wood with the tweezers. She tugged it till it came free, leaving a snail trail of blood, and Daisy let out a full-throttle banshee cry in protest, sliding off her knee and landing with a bump on the floor. She narrowed her teary eyes and yelled, "I hate you! You're the worst big sister in the world!" before running off to her bedroom.

Lily sniffled, inhaling half the carpet with her, and staggered to her feet to follow her twin. She paused only to shoot Pippa an evil look as she stalked off, saying, "This is all your fault. You should have looked after my ear muffs for me! You're a grown-up!"

Pippa closed her eyes, took a few deep breaths, and opened them again. Maybe it was all a bad dream. Maybe she'd come to and find out she was back in Kansas and her whole life hadn't blown away in a tornado after all.

No such luck. Scotty was still standing there, in his pyjamas, rocking backwards and forwards, lower lip wobbling. Oh poo! She knew what that meant. She held her arms wide and he flew into them, burrowing his small blonde head into her chest. She felt the tears well and his tiny body shake with emotion as she cuddled him close.

"I w-w-w-want B-b-b-ben!" he wailed, so upset he'd developed a brand-new stutter. He felt so fragile, so delicate, heaving with anguish in her arms and expecting her to fix it all. God, she wished she could – but she'd made a giant mess of everything and had been so utterly selfish that she'd dragged her babies down with her. They were all caught in a whirlpool of pain – and swirling right down the plughole by her side.

Pippa couldn't hold it in any more and felt her own tear ducts open up in sympathy. What a bloody disaster! Ben couldn't get out of Cornwall fast enough, both the girls hated her and Scotty was missing the only father figure he'd ever known. She couldn't even keep a pair of ear muffs safe – what hope was there for the rest of them?

"I want Ben to come home!" shouted Scotty, just in case she hadn't got the gist of it first time around.

"Darling," she said, stroking his hair back as he wiped snot all over her t-shirt, "I know exactly what you mean. Now come on, let's get you to bed."

Eventually, he'd calmed down. She'd learned that with kids emotions ran fast, furious and frenzied – but they passed quickly. She knew Lily and Daisy would forgive her in the morning. Scotty might need a bit more time, but he'd be all right. She'd have to make sure he was. It was her job and it was about time she started doing it properly again.

Yes, they were upset. But they were young, they were resilient and they were open to bribery.

She, on the other hand, felt about 108 years old as she eventually collapsed on the couch with a mug of coffee. She was covered in snot and tears – most of it Scotty's, some of it rather pathetically hers – and utterly drained, physically and emotionally.

Now the kids were finally in bed and she was finally alone, she felt weak beyond belief. While they needed her – for splinter-removal, cuddles and as an emotional punching bag – she hung on. Kept a grip on sanity. Stayed strong for them. Used the domestic carnage to block out that last view of Ben's face as he hovered by his car door: the shock, the disbelief, the...well, horror didn't feel as though it was too big a word to use. All because she'd told him she loved him. It had been so quick, so spontaneous. Just a few tiny words that came tumbling out of her mouth because she was upset. A few tiny words that had changed everything, had turned an already topsy-turvy world even more on its head.

Would she take it back, she wondered, if she found a magic time machine in the old cowshed made out of rusted tractor parts? Something HG Wells had left behind when he was in Cornwall on holiday? If she was standing there again in that field, knowing how he would react, would she still say it?

Yes. No. Maybe. Saying nothing would be the easy option. By saying nothing, she kept everything. Ben would have driven away with happy in his head and a marrow in his pants, and she would be left with the memory of that kiss and that sensational pep talk, to keep her warm at night. More importantly, if she'd kept her stupid mouth shut, he would have come back again. Back to her arms, her bed, her life. They could pick up where they left off, with the fun and the friendship and the freakily good sex. Option A – not being a complete moron – had a lot to recommend it.

But easy, she knew, wasn't always right. Wasn't always for the best. And while Option B hurt like hell, perhaps it had been needed. Things would have ended with Ben eventually. It was inevitable.

Doing it like this, at least, had been like ripping the plaster off with one short, brutal tug, instead of meandering along, on the receiving end of the emotional version of a slow, steady sandpapering to the face. It was pulling the splinter out instead of letting it fester in the flesh – and she'd expected a nine-year-old to be brave about that.

For the last few months she'd been living out a fantasy. The kids were fine, the business was doing well and even Patrick was morphing into someone new, someone better. But...there were small things wrong. Like the fact she'd forgotten to book the gas servicing for the cottage boilers; that she'd missed Scotty's check-up at the dentist; that the oil light on the Land Rover had been flashing for weeks. That she hadn't yet started panicking about her appointment with Social Services the next morning, when she normally kept several calendar days clear to practise her anxiety attacks.

Small things, but piling up. And then, she forced herself to acknowledge, there were the big things. One enormously huge thing, in fact: she was in love with a man who could never love her in return.

When it had been just about sex it had been fine. But love... well, that was right up there on the list of "important stuff to not mess up", wasn't it? She loved him. Adored him. Needed him. And in return, he...liked her. A lot, admittedly, but that wasn't enough. It would never be enough, no matter how desperately she wanted to fool herself that it was.

She deserved better than that. She deserved someone who felt exactly the same about her. That might never happen, she knew – but that wasn't an excuse for continuing to treat herself like a second-class citizen.

So, she decided, even if I do find that time machine – I wouldn't change a thing. I may feel mangled and twisted and broken beyond repair, but I will bounce back. Possibly when I'm on a zimmer frame, but I will.

As she mulled it over, examining it all in her battered mind, she even started to feel a twinge of anger. A tiny spark, which she found herself nurturing. She knew it wasn't fair, and she knew he'd always been honest, but still, it was there. Why did he have to be so screwed-up? Why did he have to cling so stubbornly to his insistence that he could never fall in love again? Why couldn't he just open his eyes and realise that they could have something truly special together? Then she wouldn't be sitting here feeling sorry for herself, she'd be doing something way more interesting, possibly involving whipped cream.

What was wrong with her? Wasn't she good enough for him? Perhaps the whole dramatic "I'll-never-love-again" routine was fake, even if he didn't realise it. A kinder way of telling her that while he was happy with the bonking, she could never be anything more.

He'd certainly been horrified enough at the thought of staying with her – from the look on his face, he'd be setting new land-speed records getting back to London. He was undoubtedly in his posh city flat right now, breathing several sighs of relief at his lucky escape. Maybe now he'd go off and find himself another Johanna, someone elegant and sophisticated and clever. Someone who knew how to do French braids and had manicures and watched art-house movies at the Barbican. Someone who didn't smell of cow shit, quite frankly.

Well, she thought, pulling herself to her weary feet to stick the kettle on again, he could sod right off. He could take his anguish and his self-pity and his drool-inducing body and stick it where... the phone! The phone was ringing!

She sprinted from the kitchen to the hall with speed that would have made Usain Bolt weep with envy, desperate to grab it before the answering machine kicked in. It could be him. It could be Ben. He could be phoning to tell her he was coming back, to swear his undying love, to make everything feel all right again. Huh, she thought, picking up the receiver – so much for that brief and unconvincing "I Am Woman" moment.

"Hello?" she said cautiously, feeling her heart squeeze so tight she thought she might choke. Please God, let it be him! Let all my stupid delusions come true. Let it be Ben.

"Miss Harte? Pippa Harte?" said an unfamiliar male voice. Disappointment washed through her like bitter coffee and she nodded before realising that the person on the other end – "he who was not Ben" – couldn't actually see her.

"Yes, speaking," she replied.

"This is Matthew Dale, I'm a reporter based in London. We've seen the photos of you and Ben Retallick and wondered if you'd like to give your side of the story at all? I'd be happy to drive over to meet you and there would, of course, be some remuneration involved – we wouldn't expect you to give up your time for nothing. I could be there first thing in the morning? We're great fans of Ben's here and I'm sure the public would be thrilled to see him happy at last..."

Pippa dropped the phone, watching but not reacting as it slithered from her hands and clattered to the stone-flagged floor. She could hear a faint tweetering noise coming from it as the reporter carried on talking. Carried on trying to convince her to splatter her whole life over the front page of a newspaper. Carried on and on and on, a disembodied voice that might just as well have been saying, "Hi – you don't know me, but I've come to completely screw your life up."

She pulled herself together, scooped it back up, and muttered a quick "no, thank you" before cutting him off.

She looked at the flashing light on the answering machine and felt terrified of what would happen if she pressed the replay button. Finger trembling, she reached out and did it anyway.

The usual series of beeps. Followed by seven messages, all from reporters, all great fans of Ben, all feeling delighted that he was happy, all wanting to pay her large sums of cash to get the inside story. All of them completely unaware of the devastation they were doling out with their breezy comments and fake bonhomie.

Shell-shocked, she left the phone off the hook. There'd be more calls, she knew, and she was in no state to deal with them.

She sat back down, booting up the old laptop, biting her lip so hard she tasted the metallic tang of fresh blood. Molluscs, poo and broomsticks! How had this happened? The day before she was due to meet with Social Services, of all days?

She waited for the page to load – the coverage of the village show on the local paper's website. Looked on in complete disbelief as she appeared across the screen in technicolour glory: pictures that had been taken of the tug of war, Ben heave-ho-ing with all his might, the crowd cheering him on, bare-chested and magnificent. One of them together afterwards, her stroking his stomach and looking at him as if he was an ice-cream sundae she was about to lick. One of them kissing, laughing, smiling. Very obviously together and not in a "just friends" kind of way.

The quality wasn't brilliant – in fact they looked as if they'd been uploaded from a mobile phone – but it didn't need to be. If pictures paint a thousand words, there was a whole graphic novel there in front of her. Her name, details about her family, where she lived and a cloying description of the "tragedy" that had taken her parents from her. No wonder those other reporters had found her so easily – the damn story gave out pretty much everything apart from sat-nav directions to the farm.

The terrible irony, she thought, as she closed the screen down, was that it was all a lie. Bad Boy Ben hadn't found love at all; he hadn't found his happy ending. He wasn't shacked up in a rural love nest with a "the brave English rose who'd won his heart". He wasn't even here any more, and, she suspected, never would be. On the very day it had all seemed to come crashing down around them, the world decided they made the perfect couple. Hah!

The list of great things about the day just kept getting longer. Anniversary of parental death. Humiliation in front of the love of her life. Said love of her life fleeing from the scene of the crime. Kids in meltdown. And now, exposed to the general public as being some kind of jailbird's harlot hours before she had to convince Margaret Dooley, her case worker, that she was a caring and responsible adult, who was perfectly capable of acting as guardian to her siblings.

Really, she thought, her head collapsing forward into her hands, could this day get any worse at all?

The minute she thought it, she wanted to take it back. Because she knew that no matter how crappy things might seem, they really can always get that little bit worse.

Right on cue, almost as though she'd provoked the universe into giving her one last poke in the ribs, there was a knock at the door.

Chapter 14

Minutes ago she'd have been hoping it was Ben. Now she feared it would be another reporter – one with a bit more gumption. If it was, she had no idea how she'd react: floods of tears or chasing them off with a pitchfork. It could go either way.

Giving in to a cowardy-custard moment, she ignored it for a minute, simply hoping it would go away – although the chances of someone accidentally knocking on the wrong door when you live six miles from the next building were extremely low.

The hammering continued and she swore, properly, before dragging her cowardy-custard feet in the direction of the door. Which wasn't even bloody locked anyway.

She opened it, expecting flash bulbs to start popping – boy, she'd look great, with her swollen eyes and snot-covered t-shirt. Instead, Mr Jensen was standing on the doorstep. Definitely not a reporter, unless he had a secret life he hadn't been telling anybody about. The "paparazzi pensioner".

"Mr Jensen!" she said, pulling the door wider. "Come in... is everything okay?"

She knew from the look on his wizened face that, no, everything wasn't okay – and realised that it must be Patrick. This time last year, pretty much all of her woes had sprung from her baby brother. Worrying about him, nagging him, borderline hating him on occasion. And she'd have been prepared for this, prepared for the inevitable trouble that followed Patrick around like a love-struck stalker.

This year, she'd slipped. Become complacent. Lulled into a false sense of security by his ever-increasing maturity, and distracted by her own pathetic love life. That's what happened when you dropped your guard: life snuck in and booted you in the face.

"It's Patrick, love," said Mr Jensen, reaching out to touch her shoulder. "He's all right, don't be panicking or anything. But he's in the hospital."

"What? Why? What happened?" she said, completely disregarding the "don't panic" part of the sentence.

"Well, he got into a fight, see, and he's a bit battered up. Nothing that time won't fix, but you should probably go and see him. I'll stay here with the kids, Pippa. Take as long as you like."

She nodded, gulping down her fear, feeling it replaced with disappointment and bitterness. Patrick. She should have known it wouldn't last. He'd been making a mess of his life for a long time now, and she was getting tired of cleaning it up – especially now, when she really needed to take a dustpan and brush to her own. It was this day. This bloody day. It was always too much for him – and this time it felt like too much for her as well.

Mr Jensen seemed to sense her reaction, or perhaps it was exactly the one he'd expected. She could now add "predictable" to her ever-growing list of character flaws.

"It wasn't his fault," he said, "not really. He'll tell you all about it, but don't be too hard on the lad – he's not all bad."

No, thought Pippa. Not all bad. Hardly a glowing recommendation was it? She scurried around looking for her bag and car keys, and did a final check on the twins and Scotty. Despite the high-octane turmoil of earlier on, all three of them were sleeping peacefully. Lily seemed to have located the missing ear muffs and was wearing them in bed.

She thanked Mr Jensen again, told him to leave the phone off the hook just in case, and ran out to the Land Rover. The oil light had gone off. Probably meant the whole thing was about to break down and need replacing with money she didn't have. She said a quick prayer to the God of Old Engines that it would, at the very least, get her to the hospital and set off.

The drive took almost an hour, even at night. One of the many joys of living in a rural community was having to travel miles to the nearest hospital. In fact, it was the same one her parents had been taken to the night they died. She shut that thought out of her mind: the last thing she needed now was to start remembering that. Remembering the way they'd looked when she confirmed it was them; sheets drawn sensitively over their bodies to hide the damage caused by both the crash and the work the medical staff had done to try and save them. If only they had. Her own life would be so very different now. She might never have met Ben and she certainly wouldn't be doing a midnight mercy mission to console her deadbeat brother.

Recognising the thought as selfish in the extreme, she adjusted her face as she walked into the side room where Patrick was being treated. She needed to pretend to be concerned, even if what she really wanted to do was smack him in the face with a wet kipper.

One look at him there, lying in the hospital's puke-green sheets, was enough to make her feel the concern for real. He was a big lad, but hospital beds have a way of making everyone look small, vulnerable. Of emphasising how ridiculously fragile we all are.

He looked up at her with two magnificent black eyes and tried to smile. His efforts were hampered by the fact that his lip was split and stitched and his nose taped up across the bony bridge that had undoubtedly been broken. He was wearing one of those gowns that shows off your bare bottom, and she could see dressings poking out of the side. His hands were scraped and scabbed and he winced when he tried to sit up.

Pippa pulled up a chair next to him, reaching out to hold one battered hand in two of hers.

"Oh dear," she said, "you won't be getting that Calvin Klein modelling job this week, will you?"

"Dunno," he replied, "this might be just the look they're going for. Farmboy chic. I'm a bit more worried I might never play the violin again..."

She smiled, looked for a place to kiss him, and realised there wasn't one. He seemed to be bruised from head to toe, the poor love. She felt a wave of guilt mainline into her like a bad drug: from the minute Mr Jensen knocked on the door, she'd done nothing but feel sorry for herself. Worry about how this affected *her*. Think about how much Patrick inconvenienced *her*. But now, seeing him lying here like this, in such pain and still trying to crack jokes, she felt terrible.

"What happened, Patrick?" she asked, not letting go of his hand, even though he was clearly seeing it as a public display of affection too far. "And stop wiggling – if I want to hold your hand, I will."

He stuck his tongue out at her. At least that wasn't bruised.

"It was Robbie and that cousin of his, Darren. They took pictures of you and Ben at the village show and sold them to the local paper. For fifty bloody quid. I mean, the fact they did it was bad enough, sis, but fifty quid? Jesus! They could at least have shown a bit more ambition. So when I found out, I was...well, a bit peed off, you might say. One thing led to another and here I am. Black and blue and two broken ribs. I'm really, really sorry. I shouldn't have lost my temper – I know you have a lot on your plate at the moment, being superwoman and all. Don't be angry with me, Pip."

There was a tremble in that last plea that broke her heart. Eighteen years old, but still a baby.

"I'll be angry with you when you're better," she said, "all right? It'd be no fun picking on you in this state. But now I just want you to concentrate on getting out of here. You're a big strong lummox. It'll take more than a beating to knock any sense into you. And... well, thank you. For defending my honour and all that."

She realised that her eyes were filling up with her apparently never-ending supply of tears, and wasn't quite sure why. It had been a day of too much everything.

"You all right, Pip?" said Patrick, struggling to sit up with his injuries. "Why are you crying? You never cry! Is it because of the reporters? Or Social Services? Or Mum and Dad?"

"Ha! I seem to do nothing but cry at the moment," she replied, wiping the silly tears away – it really was pathetic. He was the one lying there in pain, not her. "It's like I've stored it all up just for today...and to answer your question, all of the above and more. It's...Ben. I don't think he'll be coming back, Patrick."

"Why?" he asked, frowning so hard his scabs collided.

"Well. That's complicated. But mainly because I said I...because I told him that...I told him that I..."

"Bloody hell. Did you drop the L-Bomb on him, sis? Is that what it is?"

Against all the odds, Pippa laughed – he'd always had a great way with words, her Patrick.

"Yep. I dropped the L-Bomb. And he did a runner to escape the blast. And that's that! So now I'm going to forget all about him, put my Superwoman costume back on and concentrate on sorting you lot out instead. I mean, look what happens to you the minute I turn my back!"

"Sounds good. But Pip…"

"Yes?"

"The man's a prat. He doesn't deserve you. Neither do I. 'Nuff said."

Ben turned over in his bed for what felt like the millionth time that night. He stared at the numbers on the digital clock, glaring out at him from the bedside table. It was still only 2.34am. Precisely three minutes later than the last time he looked.

He gave up, threw off the sheets and went in search of coffee. Caffeine was always the perfect cure for insomnia, he thought.

He padded barefoot into the kitchen and set the water to boil. He glanced around, realised the whole place was layered with dust, with a pinch of neglect thrown in. He hadn't been back here for so long he'd forgotten how little he actually liked it.

The flat was another remnant from his old life. He'd bought it because it was in the right area, the right part of town. Because it fitted in with everything he thought he was and everything he thought he aspired to be. A bit like Johanna – and only slightly more expensive.

Now the chrome fittings and stylish furniture just annoyed him. It was all so...sterile. Everything worked perfectly – everything looked good. None of the tiles was cracked, there were no squeaky floorboards. But none of it felt right. In fact, nothing felt right – and he wasn't so much of an idiot that he didn't know why.

He'd only been away from Harte Farm for half a day and already he was missing it. Missing the chaos and the clutter of the kids. The comedy noises of the animals. The clean air, the roads that stretched for miles down to the sea. And mainly, of course, he was missing her. His Pippa.

When she'd told him she loved him, with him hovering half in, half out of his car, he'd been so shocked he couldn't even respond. Even now, he had no idea how he should have responded – but looking like a brain-damaged guppy probably wasn't high up on the list of options.

He could, of course, have got back out of the car and been a man about it. Had the conversation that needed to be had. Delayed his meeting and sorted out his priorities. He could also have followed her back over the car park, caught up with her and apologised. He could even have done what he now realised – after several hours of Congestion Charge hell, stale coffee and his own company – he really should have done a long time ago: taken her in his arms and told her he loved her too.

Because he did, of course he did. How could he not love her? She was perfectly lovable in every single way. It had just taken her bravery to push the issue out into the open. Big Bad Ben, shown up as the coward he was by a girl who should be barely out of university.

He could be there right now, with her. Feeling the silk of her hair in his hands. Feeling her slender curves move beneath him. Hearing her moan in pleasure, and then afterwards holding her in his arms and telling her he loved her. Over and over again, to make up for the fact that it had taken him so long to admit it to himself.

Instead, he'd been a great big idiot. Caught unawares and displaying the usual artless male reaction to a crying woman, he'd run away. There was really no other way to put it. He'd run away like the tool he was.

He'd been trying to call her all night, but her phone had been constantly engaged. To start with, he hoped she'd call him – then he realised she didn't have his landline. He'd gone ex-directory to avoid reporters as soon as he'd got out of jail, and had never given her the number. He'd tried her mobile and texted, but never heard back. And after checking his every two minutes, as well as charging it up just in case, he'd had to accept that he wasn't going to hear back from her.

And you know what? It was nothing more than he deserved.

He drained the last dregs of the almost undrinkable coffee and made a decision. He'd go to his meeting in the morning – he really did need to sort the book stuff out – and then he'd drive all the way back down to Cornwall. If he was going to tell Pippa that he loved her, if he was going to take that huge leap of faith that he'd been convinced he'd never take again, then he'd do it in person.

He might even make an appointment with an estate agent first, look at putting this place on the market. Whatever happened with Pippa, he wanted out.

Okay, he thought, rubbing his sleep-starved eyes, that's a plan. Sort out career. Sell flat. Drive for five hours. Persuade Pippa to marry me.

Easy.

Chapter 15

"I've had some very pleasing reports from the school about Scotty, Lily and Daisy," said Margaret Dooley, adjusting her glasses and looking up at Pippa across her desk.

She'd always reminded Pippa of an owl. An owl that had the capacity to take her children away and place them in foster homes. That kind of owl.

She was actually a nice lady, and had been the one who'd decided to give Pippa a shot at the whole mothering lark in the first place – so big bonus points there. But still, having to present herself four times a year and go through the endless checks and interviews, the constant testing, left little room for kind thoughts. Pippa knew it was right – knew that the welfare of the kids had to come first – but it still stung. And today, of all days, it stung like a whole army of wasps. With hangovers.

Sadly, no matter how nice she was, Margaret Dooley would always be The Enemy. It wasn't fair, but it was how she felt.

Pippa so didn't want to be there, in that stuffy, overcrowded little office, knowing that everything she said and everything she did was being weighed and valued. That she needed to look neat and tidy, respond calmly and appear completely in control of not only her own destiny, but that of three small children as well. In short, she had to act like a grown-up, even if she felt like a blubbering baby herself.

That was difficult enough at the best of times, but as she'd only managed about three hours' sleep, had a brother in hospital, was being pursued by every journalist in Britain and also had – oh yes – a completely shattered heart to deal with, this was even more testing than usual.

"That's great," said Pippa, smiling so hard she thought her face might break. "They're all doing really well at home too."

"Wonderful," said Mrs Dooley, flipping through a few more sheets of paper. The file was huge, brown manila, stuffed with sheets and paperclipped documents, photocopies and pictures. Years' worth of assessments just like this one. It was probably all on computer somewhere or other, floating around in cyber space, but seeing it there on the desk – big enough to sink the Titanic – always made Pippa feel depressed.

"What about Patrick?" Mrs Dooley asked after a few moments of silence. Pippa had already decided to take the obvious route out of that one and lie. As Patrick was now technically an adult anyway, it didn't really matter. Margaret had interviewed him several times over the years; most of that bloody file was probably made up of his sarcastic comments, police interaction and anger-management issues.

"He's doing well, thank you. Had a little accident yesterday, but nothing serious. In fact he's been doing some volunteer work in the community," she said. Admittedly, he was forced into it after wrecking a war veteran's home, but that seemed a petty thing to mention. All's well that ends well.

"And he's applying to agricultural college too," she added. Just for luck. That one was at least kind of true.

"I see. Well, that is good news. And you, Pippa. How are you doing?"

Ah. Here it came, just like it always did. The part where Margaret Dooley's little owl face went all serious and scrunchy, as she started to probe and poke and make sure Pippa was "coping with her challenges". The part where her glasses were lowered and she stared at her with that earnest expression.

If only she knew how many challenges there were, Pippa thought. As usual, she smiled and assured her that everything was fine. Perfect. Lovely. She was the happiest, most capable person in the whole wide world. Assuming that everyone else was dead!

Margaret nodded, glasses wobbling, and closed the file quite abruptly. It made a kind of small thud and Pippa jumped at the sound. Nervous? Not at all.

"I couldn't help but see the news, Pippa, about you and your gentleman friend. I wasn't snooping – it has been all over the papers this morning, after all. Is there anything I should know?"

Pippa felt as if she'd swallowed a bullfrog and she screwed up her eyes to try and ward off a descending panic attack. She clenched her fists together so hard her nails started to cut into the soft flesh of her palms.

She'd known this might be coming. Margaret Dooley would have had to have been living on Mars to have missed out on Pippa's new-found celebrity. She'd prepared a speech. Knew exactly what she was going to say. How she was going to explain that the papers had misinterpreted it; that she hadn't actually invited a convicted violent criminal into the family home she shared with three young children...except, of course, that's exactly what she *had* done. It just didn't look so good in black and white.

She'd never felt any threat from Ben; never seen him as a violent man. All of her instincts had told her that he was a safe person to have around her children. And...well, they loved him. The irony was that while she'd given a lot of thought to that aspect of his continued presence in their lives, she'd missed out on the risk assessment about how he could potentially mess them up in different ways. Like forcing her to fall in love with him, working his way into the kids' affections, then leaving at the first sign of commitment. Slight oversight, that.

"Um..." she said, realising that Mrs Dooley was still waiting for an answer. Bugger. Where was that speech she'd prepared? Had the bullfrog eaten it?

"Before you answer, Pippa, let me state for the record that you are perfectly entitled to a private life. Mr Retallick's case is well known, and although I've never met the man personally, he has paid his debt to society. His conviction had no relation to child-protection issues, and as far as I am concerned you are mature enough to make your own decisions. If, however, the relationship reaches the stage where Mr Retallick would, for example, move into the family home, then he would need to come in here and be assessed, and also be present at future meetings. Does that sound fair?"

Fair. Yes. It sounded fair, thought Pippa. And also completely, totally, one hundred per cent irrelevant. Because Ben was gone – he was out of Cornwall, out of their lives and out of chances. The thought of going through all of this again – being questioned about her sex life by a middle-aged owl – made her feel sick.

"Thank you for that, Mrs Dooley. But I can assure you that isn't going to happen. I can't deny knowing Mr Retallick, but the stories in the newspapers are vastly exaggerated. He is no longer staying at Harte Farm and has returned to London – where I presume he will stay. He has had very limited contact with the children, and will, in future, have none at all."

Okay, that was another lie, she thought, but one that God would definitely forgive her for. He had, of course, had a lot of contact with the children. So much so that Scotty was still crying for him this morning as she drove him to school. But the rest? That was true. He was gone and he wasn't coming back.

Mrs Dooley nodded, not looking entirely convinced, but letting the subject drop.

"Then that's fine, Pippa. I think that's all for this time. I'll see you again in three months, and as ever, if you need any help at all in the meantime, please don't hesitate to contact me."

Oh yeah, thought Pippa, standing to shake her hand, I'll do that. I'll call you at 3am when I'm still crying over my lost love, and I'll ask you to pick the kids up from school when the car's finally packed in, and I'll tap you up for your credit card so I can pay the bloody vet's bill. Not. In fact, she was determined never to ask anyone for help ever again – she'd started to depend on Ben, without even noticing it, and look where that had got her.

I'm better off alone, she thought, on the drive home. At least when I'm alone, I know what's required of me, even if I don't feel like I can do it all. I know that it's me who has to fix the gatepost and muck out the animals and do the school run and look after the guests and try to remember the homework and everything else that needs to be ticked off a list.

It was a lot of stuff to manage – but as she now wouldn't be spending half her day getting sumptuously sexed up, she'd have a lot more time on her hands. She'd let Ben get too close to all of them, take up too big a space in all their lives – and she had nobody to blame but herself.

It had to end – the tears, the self-pity, the weakness that swamped her when she thought about him. It had to end. Right now. Life went on after she lost her parents and life would go on after losing Ben.

This, she thought, jumping out of the Land Rover as she pulled up in the driveway, is the new me. Lone mama wolf, all the way. Alpha female. Leader of the pack. She even gave a little howl to cheer herself up as she went.

Sadly, the howl turned into a yelp as she noticed she wasn't alone. Ben's sleek Audi was parked down the side of the house and the man himself was perched on the fence, wearing the same walking boots and anorak he'd been wearing the first day he arrived. It felt like a lifetime ago. When she was a different person, a stronger person.

She froze as he jumped down from the fence and started to walk towards her. He was smiling, but seemed nervous. Tense. His fists were clenched at his sides and his hair was curling on his forehead, damp from the drizzle that had been falling all day. Summer had gone, in all kinds of ways.

By the time he reached her, Pippa had retreated all the way back to the Land Rover and was hovering by the door as though she was considering getting back in. Maybe she should, she thought. Get right back in, lock the doors against the love zombie attack and drive the hell out of Dodge. Funny how fast her feelings had changed. Not that long ago she'd wanted nothing more than to be back in his arms. Now she was scared. Angry. Wishing she had a "cloak of invisibility" she could wrap around herself.

She'd spent the drive home giving herself a pep talk that almost – almost – started to convince her that she was ready to go it alone – and stay alone. Which was a heck of a lot easier when you had no choice in the matter – and decidedly harder with the man himself standing in front of you, looking like he'd swallowed his own bullfrog.

Ben sensed her tension and stopped a few feet away, one hand reaching out towards her, drifting slowly in the empty space between them. She didn't know whether she wanted to take hold and kiss it or stab it with a fork.

"Pippa," he said, simply. "We need to talk..."

This was it, he thought. Just do it. Don't wait for the perfect moment – it might never arrive. Just tell her you're sorry. Tell her you love her. Tell her you want to spend the rest of your life with her. Tell her you've never felt anything like this in your entire sorry existence and you never want it to end.

Except...her face. She looked different. Older, as though she'd aged a decade overnight. She was backing off as though she was terrified of him, as though she might run like a spooked puppy if he went any closer. Wow! He'd really done a number on her.

"No," she said, straightening up, as though she realised how weak she looked, cowering by the car, and had made an active decision to change that.

"No, we don't, Ben," she repeated, louder now, holding her head high, fighting to control the quavering in her lower lip. "The time for talking has gone. I was stupid to say what I did yesterday and I don't think I even meant it. I was just emotional, overwhelmed with everything, thinking about my parents. I've had time since to think about it all – when I wasn't fielding off journalists, that is, or dealing with Social Services quizzing me about my sex life."

"What do you mean, journalists?" he asked, frowning. He'd noticed a few funny looks at his meeting that morning, but hadn't made the connection. And as nobody had his new numbers, they'd been unable to contact him. He'd got into the habit of avoiding the media at all costs over the last year, not wanting to see what anybody had to say about him.

"Journalists. You know, people who write for newspapers, blogs, that kind of thing?" she snapped, marching towards the house ahead of him, wielding her keys like a samurai sword she was considering using on his neck. "We hit the headlines after the village show, and I've been enjoying my fifteen minutes of fame. Are you coming in or not? I don't have time to stand in the rain and get a cold."

He followed, his head whirling. God, he'd been so stupid. Forgotten what could happen – and how it could drag her down with him. He'd been so arrogant, prancing around without his shirt on, taking part in the tug of bloody war, kissing Pippa in public. Behaving as though he was a normal person, who was entitled to a normal life. He wasn't – and living his fantasy countryside concoction with Pippa had made him forget that, however briefly. He'd felt safe here, with her – something about the distance and the sea and the kids and the farm and the...well, the sex. None of it had felt like the life he'd left behind.

Now, he could tell, she'd paid the price for that temporary insanity. He'd never forgive himself if it had affected her meeting with Social Services. If there was any chance the kids could be taken from her because of him...

Was there a way to make it right? Could she forgive him? Could they find a way through it? He could only hope that the damage he'd caused wasn't enough to destroy everything she'd worked for, and everything they'd had together. Everything he hoped they might still have. Whatever he needed to do – however much he needed to apologise, to humble himself – he'd do it. If he needed to plead his case with Social Services, wear an ankle bracelet, install a GPS tracking device – anything. He'd do it. Pippa was worth jumping through any hoops that were put in front of him – if only she could still love him. If only she was lying about it all being a mistake.

He followed her into the kitchen, watching as she went about her business, buzzing with tension. She filled the kettle with water. Switched it on. Switched it off again. Stared at it, wondering why it wasn't working, then flipped the button once more when she figured it out. Got two mugs from the cupboard and immediately dropped one on to the hard stone flags, where it shattered into what looked like a million tiny pieces.

"Oh rubber ducks!" she said, squatting down to collect up the shards.

"Let me help," he said, kneeling beside her, trying to push her trembling hands away from the mess she'd made. The mess he'd made.

"No!" she shrieked, shoving his fingers away. "I don't need your help! Not with this, not with anything – I don't need anyone's help, do you understand?"

He looked at her clenched fists, the slender shoulders that were shaking with uncontrolled emotion. Blonde hair that seemed to fizz around her face as though she was plugged into a socket. The tears casting a glassy sheen over the blue of her eyes. She was angry and tense and closed off in a way he'd never seen before. He'd taken this free-spirited, generous, kind-hearted savage and broken her.

So, yes, he understood. He understood that he was, just like she'd told him all that time ago, a perfect moron.

Ben reached out, grabbed hold of her hand and held it in both of his. He wouldn't let go, no matter how hard she struggled. He tugged her towards him sharply and they both fell, unbalanced, to the floor. He held her in his arms, shielding her body from the sharp slivers of china, and pressed her head against his chest, using his bulk to hold her there as she tried to wriggle free.

After an undignified minute of pointless struggle, she gave up. Sobbed and collapsed into him, ear set against the thudding of his heart. She lay still and shaken as he twined his fingers into her hair, kissed her face, murmured to her that everything would be all right. She took a moment to let the familiar feeling of comfort flow through her: she was in Ben's arms. She could smell Ben's scent. She could feel Ben's breath against her. For that one blessed moment she allowed herself the briefest of fantasies that she could stay there. That while he was with her, everything really would be all right. That she was safe and secure and they would both live happily ever after.

All too quickly, that moment was gone. Replaced with something deeper and darker and altogether more depressing: reality.

"Let me go, Ben," she said quietly. She knew she couldn't force him to release her – he was too strong. But she also knew that he would never hurt her – not that way, at least. As for the other ways? Well, the damage was already done there. "Please let me go," she repeated.

"I don't want to," he muttered, his nose buried in her hair, inhaling the lavender, refusing to budge.

"But I want you to," she insisted, a note of steel creeping into her voice. "I want you to let me go and then I want you to leave. And I don't want you to ever come back. I don't love you. You don't love me. I know that now. I don't love you and I don't need you, and it's time for us both to go back to our real lives."

Ben felt her words smash into his soul like an anvil, crushing all his hope, all his dreams. He wanted to argue. To tell her he knew she was lying. To convince her to give him – to give them – another chance. But he looked at her face and he saw truth. He saw determination. He saw the kind of blunt rejection that he'd never wanted to see on a woman's face ever again. The same closed, cold look that Johanna had used when she'd cut him out of her life just as ruthlessly. In his mind, the two even flickered together, Johanna's face shadowed with Pippa's. Two different women: exactly the same result. Neither of them wanted him. He'd offered them both his heart and they'd both said no.

He closed his eyes, refusing to cry, even though part of him wanted to. Wanted to weep and sob and throw himself at Pippa's feet and beg her to keep him. Just like he had with Johanna – minutes before she walked out of the door.

No. Never. He wouldn't do it again. It didn't work that time and it wouldn't work this time, he knew.

Slowly, silently, he disentangled himself from Pippa, laying her safely back down on the floor, alone.

She looked up, lying there on the cold stone flags, surrounded by shattered pieces of pottery, and watched as he walked, wordlessly, away. Out of the door. Out of her life.

Chapter 16

"This," said Pippa, to the cow's backside, "is ridiculous, isn't it?"

SpongeBob gave out a low, bone-jarring moo and turned around to stare at her with luminous brown eyes.

"I'm glad you agree," Pippa replied, giving her a friendly slap on the flanks as she finished the milking. It only seemed polite to make conversation when you had your hands on a lady's udders. A bit like when you were at the hairdresser's and they asked if you were going anywhere nice on holiday.

In the old days, when the farm was worked, there'd been all kinds of machinery installed to do it for them – but with only SpongeBob left it wasn't worth the money or the effort. Instead, Pippa had to get up close and personal. Non-stop glamour.

But since the kids had gone back to school after the summer holidays and Patrick had gone off to college, it often represented the only adult conversation she had all day. Even if it was a bovine adult.

Job done, Pippa stayed where she was, perched on her stool, as SpongeBob ambled over to the feeding trough. Obviously not in the mood for a long chat – or possibly just bored at the predictable topic.

Pippa was even starting to feel a bit bored with it herself, and the fact that she was asking a dairy cow for advice was proof of just how low she'd sunk. But...well, she didn't have anyone else to ask. Anyone who'd say what she wanted to hear anyway, which she supposed was different. SpongeBob – due to the language barrier – always said exactly what she wanted to hear, which made a pleasant change.

Three months had passed since Ben had left. Life, such as it was, had resumed business as usual. Patrick was discharged from the hospital after a couple of days, battered, bruised, but none the worse for wear. In fact, he'd used the whole escapade to his advantage with Gemma, the barmaid they always described as "new" no matter how long she'd been there. Gemma had been oddly impressed with his war wounds and had become a semi-permanent fixture in his life. As permanent as anything when it came to an eighteen-year-old's love life, anyway.

Pippa had made it clear that she didn't want her staying over – definitely no more sleepovers of any kind, thank you very much – but Patrick went to her flat over the pub several times a week. He even texted her to say he was going, which marked a major leap forward in his behaviour. And when she had time off, Gemma visited him in Truro, where he was now studying.

It was, in an icky-yucky-how-can-you-fancy-my-brother way, kind of sweet.

Scotty still asked for Ben occasionally, especially when he was upset at some major disaster, like stubbing his toe or forgetting his line in the school assembly. But it was less frequent and less vocal and less often accompanied by howling tears and snot storms. Lily and Daisy still pined a little and Pippa knew when they were talking about him – because they did it in their old "secret" language, huddled in the corner of the kitchen, looking shifty. Even at their age, they'd picked up enough girl savvy to know it might upset their sister if they did it in the open.

The journalists had, slowly but surely, taken "no" for an answer – made so much easier by the fact that he was very obviously not there, and had, in fact, started to do a few interviews in advance of his book coming out. She was no longer news and was able to return to normal.

Huh. Normal, she thought, squelching through the mud in her wellies, fresh milk sloshing in its bucket. As normal as she ever got, anyway.

Her last meeting with Mrs Dooley had gone well, apart from one brief interlude where she insisted Pippa looked "less than herself", and asked several piercing questions about her health and state of mind. It had felt uncomfortable, even more so than usual, and she knew exactly what she was getting at.

She'd lost weight – there was way too much room in her jeans these days – and seemed to have somehow...deflated. Life hadn't exactly been a laugh a minute before, but after? It was, well, grim. Every day felt like a slog. Every night seemed to last forever. She was tortured by dreams in the same way she had been for the year after her parents died: terrible dreams that told lies; dreams about being with him, being happy, feeling the touch of his lips on hers, hearing the sound of his voice, lying safe in his arms.

Every time it happened, she woke up in a momentary glow of contentment – until reality hit and the world tumbled back down around her shoulders. It hurt, more than she could ever have imagined something as trivial as lost love could. For the first time, she started to think there might be some truth in the concept of "a broken heart".

Summer had been tough – kids off school, all the cottages full. Having to service Honeysuckle every time guests left, swamped with memories, the ghosts of lovers past. The toilet had even blocked again and she fixed it in floods of tears, chiding herself for being so stupid.

So, yes, Mrs Dooley had a point. But what could she do about it? It's not like she wasn't trying. She wasn't wallowing or deliberately visiting him in her nocturnal subconscious – it just happened.

She'd assured the concerned case worker that everything was fine, bluffed her way through it until Mrs Dooley couldn't continue to probe without being downright rude.

Sadly, she wasn't the only one. Patrick was obviously worried and spent an unhealthy amount of time calling home – often drunk, which was reassuring at least – to check up on her. He'd even enlisted Mr Jensen, who repeatedly phoned and asked her for help she knew he didn't need. She'd call round with a box of tea bags for him and then discover several boxes stashed in the kitchen cupboard when she put them away and one time he'd begged her for a lift to the doctor's because his car was out of tax – and yet funnily enough, when she'd glanced in the windscreen, it had two months left to run.

It was a conspiracy. They were all ganging up on her and she didn't especially like it. She knew their intentions were good – Mrs Dooley, Mr Jensen, even Patrick – but it made her feel like a victim, someone who needed to be cosseted and cared for and treated with kid gloves. And as she'd spent the last three years being the one who held the thread of their strange-shaped little family together, it wasn't a role that sat well with her.

Now, though, with Patrick gone, the kids in school, and no more guests for a fortnight, she felt like she'd welcome a bit of cosseting. Or a bit of distraction at least.

Because the package that had arrived in the post yesterday had had a similar effect to unwrapping one of those cartoon bombs with a lit fuse sticking out of it. And she had nobody – bar the less-than- chatty SpongeBob – to talk to about it.

The postman had smiled and chatted as she signed and she hadn't really given it much thought. Suppliers often sent her catalogues to look at or samples of the sumptuous holiday-home decor she could buy if she ever had two sixpences to rub together. She'd assumed it would be that – some chintzy country-curtain swatches or a glossy set of back copies of travel magazines she could never afford to advertise in. The kind that Tregowan Lodge used.

She'd opened it over her third coffee of the day, which she ended up wearing as soon as she realised who it was from.

Cursing, she'd jumped up, grabbed some kitchen roll and started to mop up the mess, squelching the soggy paper down over the spreading puddle of steaming brown liquid before it had time to reach the pages of the book.

The book that Ben had sent her. She knew it was from him because it had "by Ben Retallick" all over the front cover, which had allowed her lightning detection skills to piece it together. A hardback, the dust jacket all done in moody midnight blues and blacks, bare branches drenched in sinister moonlight. *Fear No Evil*, it was called. But she'd known that. They'd talked about his book, his writing, and she already knew how the story ended. Pretty much everyone died, apart from the hard-boiled cop and the feisty prosecution lawyer he'd fallen for. Cheerful stuff.

She reached out with a scalded finger and poked it, as if it might come to life, or open up and unleash a Princess Leia-style hologram of a full-sized Ben Retallick. That, her nerves really couldn't take.

There was a note tucked inside the sleeve and she tugged it out gingerly. Without planning it – because really, who would plan to do such a lame thing? – she picked it up and sniffed it. As though over the several days and hundreds of miles that it had travelled, that tiny handwritten note would still somehow retain the scent of him.

Unsurprisingly, it didn't, so she resorted to more traditional means of communication and read the note rather than inhaling it.

"Dear Pippa," it started, "I thought you might be interested in this. Most of the follow-up was written while I was with you in Cornwall and will forever be associated with that time in my mind. Hopefully yours as well. This is an advance copy – the book will be launched at a party this Saturday in London. I've written the details on the back. I'd love to see you there, but if you're too busy with Patrick, Lily, Scotty, SpongeBob, Harry Potter and Phineas and Ferb, I do understand and wish you all the best."

It was signed simply "Ben". No love or kisses or XOXOXOs. Just Ben. Just Ben, who'd won her over that very first day by remembering all of those names and who still remembered them now. Just Ben. The man from the duck pond.

And "just Ben", she realised, was more than enough to shatter any attempts at calm she'd managed to fake over the last few months.

Her initial reaction was panic, followed by anger, followed by sadness, followed by more panic. He made it sound so easy – "I'd love to see you there". As though she could simply dump the kids, jump on a train and go to a posh London publishing party. As though that was even remotely possible in her reality.

For a start, she'd stick out like a sore thumb in that kind of crowd. She had nothing to wear, obviously. And even more obviously – she couldn't face him. Couldn't bear to see him surrounded by his glamorous London friends, making small talk, flirting and laughing and possibly having full-blown sex with gorgeous crime thriller groupies on the book signing table...okay, that last one was a stretch, but still. The fact remained.

She couldn't.

Chapter 17

"You can, and you are," said Patrick when he'd turned up on Saturday morning.

"I don't want to go, Patrick, and I wish I'd never even told you. It was a moment of weakness."

"It was a moment of drunkenness actually, sis, and don't try to deny it. Made a pleasant change to be on the receiving end for a change."

Pippa felt herself flush slightly at the accusation and wished she could argue the point – but it was true. Shaken and stirred – just like a Martini that James Bond wouldn't drink – she'd cracked that night, after the kids were in bed and tucked in to the Christmas sherry that had been there for the last two years. It tasted vile and she probably had some kind of blood poisoning, but it had done the job. Temporary oblivion. Phones, she thought, should come with breathalysers attached.

"Anyway," said Patrick, "I think you actually do want to go. I think the fact you told me was your subconscious's way of admitting it. You knew I'd come home – even I'm not so much of a waste of space that I wouldn't. You've been miserable as sin since he left and I'm fed up of worrying about you. I know you did it for years with me, but I'm not as good a person as you are and it sucks."

"My subconscious? What the hell are you studying and what does that have to do with animal husbandry?" she snapped, angry with him. With herself. With the knowledge that he'd nailed it one hundred per cent. What right did he have to go all perceptive on her now, when she least needed it?

"You and Ben have quite a lot to do with animal husbandry, if I remember rightly... now come on, get your stuff together and I'll run you to the station. I know it's hard. I know you're scared. But you've been limping along for months now – don't you think it's worth a chance? You never gave up on us, Pip – so don't give up on yourself."

His tone was harsh, but the words melted her into goo. She felt tears stinging the back of her tired eyeballs and knew he was right… Again. This was starting to turn into a very annoying habit of his, she thought, as she reluctantly packed an overnight bag. She *had* given up on herself. And she'd only been half alive for the last three months, like an electrical appliance on standby. Waiting for someone to come along and turn her on...she giggled at the wordplay and wondered if that sherry was still in her system. It probably had the half-life of a decade. She'd be drunk for years.

She'd tried really hard to adjust, to keep calm and carry on. To go back to the way she'd been in the era she thought of as BB – Before Ben. To pick up the threads of her chaotic-yet-ordered life, and pretend he'd never existed, never hurt her as badly as he had. To fool herself and her body into believing that the busy-ness of everyday life in Pippa-land was enough to keep her occupied, keep her fulfilled.

In reality, he'd never left her mind. He'd taken up a huge parking space in her heart and there didn't seem to be any way of moving him on. So she had two choices. Plod through the rest of her life feeling like an extra from a horror film or take the plunge. Right now both felt equally as frightening.

He'd made the first contact. He'd invited her back into his life. Now she had to be brave enough to take the next step, even if she felt about as brave as the Cowardly Lion before he bumped into Dorothy. It felt like having a lung transplant without the anaesthetic.

By the time she was standing outside the restaurant – a mere six hours of public-transport hell later – she felt even worse. From an initial sense of resolve, she'd descended into a blancmange of self-doubt. What if he was just inviting her to be polite? What if he just felt guilty and wanted to say goodbye properly? What if he'd been seeing a therapist, who'd told him to find some closure?

What if – and this was the one that killed her – he'd found someone else? It had been three months. Okay, she hadn't met anyone, but that wasn't surprising. The only new man who'd come into her life had been about seventy-eight and wielding a giant lollipop stick at the school crossing. The-middle-of-nowhere, Cornwall, was hardly dating central.

But his life was different. It was big, it was glitzy, it probably involved non-stop invitations to Chelsea sex parties and floozies throwing themselves into his arms as he did his shopping in Waitrose. He was gorgeous, he was successful, he was kind of famous. He was, in every way, an "eligible bachelor".

Yes, she thought, staring through the windows of the restaurant to try and get a glimpse of him with his fictional new fiancée, he was probably taken by now.

The nights were starting to draw in as autumn arrived, and although the air still felt warm, the skies were darkening around her. The street – tucked away in a part of town where the houses were all big and white and expensive – was bustling, people spilling in and out of cafés and bars, chatting and laughing and acting like the world wasn't about to end.

Inside, she could see dim lighting, moody decorations, waiting staff dressed in black and white walking round with trays of booze and the kind of nibble food that taunted your taste buds. There was a piano, a man in a suit playing it. Crowds of nicely dressed people talking and smiling around small tables piled high with copies of Ben's books. Some of them were holding them up, examining them and discussing them.

It looked like an alien moonscape to Pippa, standing outside in her best pair of jeans and a new top she'd found time to buy before she left. Okay, it had cost £9.99 from Primark, but it was new and it was the best she had. The little black dress had been a no-no – too big these days and also too laden with memories.

Now, standing outside and not knowing if she'd ever find the courage to walk in, she felt ridiculously young and ridiculously scruffy and...well, just ridiculous in every way. This wasn't her life. This wasn't her world. And if the two collided, her head might literally explode all over the canapés.

She screwed up her eyes to see better through the window, taking one last glance before she left. Before she got the Tube to the cheap hotel she'd booked and raided the mini-bar, launching her new life as a lush. She'd tried to be brave. Tried to take the next step. But it was all too much. All too scary.

She leaned into the pane, shielding her eyes as she squinted through. Maybe she'd get one little glimpse of him. One little glimpse to last the rest of her life.

The door opened and the sounds of the piano and the chat and the world that wasn't hers spilled out onto the pavement in a small aural wave. She jumped away from the window, leaving her breath smeared on it, like a guilty child caught sneaking a look at the Christmas presents.

"Pippa?" he said, taking a hesitant step towards her. "Is that you?"

Ben. Of course. How silly of her to forget that you could actually see through glass in both directions. She must have looked like a prize pillock for the last few minutes.

"Um...yes. Who else would be out here sniffing the window pane?" she said, shuffling nervously, wishing the cobbled mews street would open up and swallow her whole.

She looked up at him and her heart thudded so heavily, so slowly that she thought it might actually stop. Even in the shadows, she could see how amazing he looked, dressed in a sharp black suit and a brilliant white shirt, open a few buttons at the neck. His hair had been cut and no longer flopped over his forehead, but she could still make out the luscious dark waves and remember how they'd felt. His jacket accentuated the breadth of his shoulders and his legs seemed to go on forever, down to his smartly shined shoes. He looked like someone from a movie. Male lead, action hero, life-saving paediatrician, prize-winning scientist, all rolled into one. Just Ben, my arse, she thought.

She, on the other hand, looked like a Victorian urchin about to go and ask for an extra bowl of gruel. God! Sometimes life just wasn't fair.

She took a step back, considering making a run for it. Simply turning around and legging it, as fast as she could, as far as she could. He'd never catch her. Not in those shoes.

"Please, don't go!" he said, reaching out and touching her arm. "Come inside. We need to talk – we both do."

No, she thought, I don't need to talk. I need to escape and drink and pass out and wake up needing nothing more than a couple of paracetamol. But she didn't fight him as he guided her through the door, keeping a firm grip on her hand, as if she was a nervous race horse and he was the whisperer. The door closed to behind her and she found herself enveloped in that moody lighting, the sound of the piano, the low hum of chatter all around her.

She stood huddled in on herself, as though if she tried hard enough and wrapped her arms tight enough around her own body, no one would notice she was there. Ben looked at her, so scared, so small and felt the heft of his guilt come crashing in. She'd lost weight. There were dark circles under her eyes that told him she hadn't been sleeping. She was wearing a new top, with the price tag still hanging from the hem without her noticing. She was a shadow of the Pippa he'd first met, so vital and young and full of energy. He couldn't imagine how much it had cost her, emotionally, to come here and see him.

He'd done this to her. And now it was his job to fix it.

"Pippa," he said, suddenly aware of his own fatigue, his own nerves, "I need to tell you something. I need to tell you that –"

He stopped as the door to the restaurant slammed open, shoved so hard it banged back against the wall with a loud thud. There was a sudden lull in the conversation as everyone turned around to see what the interruption was, such an impolite noise against the genteel backdrop.

Like everyone else, Pippa looked up. Saw the door still quaking on its hinges. Saw the man who'd kicked it open – and recognised him as Darren McConnell, the man who Ben had attacked. Admittedly he didn't have the bandages and the broken nose any more, but she still recognised him. A small woman followed him, dressed in a tube dress covered in sequins. She was trying to hold on to his arm, to restrain him, but he slapped her hand away.

He steamed through the door and right towards them. A few people looked up and over, and Pippa saw other people's faces pull the same expression of shock that she knew she was wearing as well. Next to her, Ben stood up, tall and tense, a deep frown crossing his forehead.

McConnell was small – next to Ben, anyway – and he had to stand up on his tiptoes to get his face up close, his already ferret-like features contorted with sly aggression.

"Read about this in the papers," he said, sneering. "Thought I'd show me face. In a way, this is all down to me, isn't it? I was the – what do you call it – the catapult? Nah... that's not it... the catalyst! Yeah, that's it. If it weren't for me, you'd never have written a bloody book, would you?"

The woman stayed a few steps behind him, the way she was hunched in on herself showing she was embarrassed. Scared. Trying not to be noticed.

Ben took a step back and Pippa could see the effort he was making to stay calm. To stay in control. To keep his hands in tight fists by his sides. She touched his arm, reminding him she was there. Wanting him to win that battle – because calm was the only way to go.

"This is an invite-only event, McConnell," he finally said, his voice a low growl. "And you're not invited. Leave. Now."

"I thought my invite must have got lost in the post," McConnell replied, casting a sideways glance at Pippa. He looked her up and down and smirked at her.

"Who's this, then? That bird I read about? She's nothing to write home about, mate...thought you could have done better for yourself. Like my Shelley here."

Pippa glanced in the direction of the shivering Shelley and their eyes briefly met. Exchanged looks of mutual sympathy and barely controlled anxiety. Poor cow, thought Pippa. What a life he must lead her, and she probably didn't even have a SpongeBob to talk to about it.

McConnell was edging forward, getting more in Ben's face, his voice getting louder with every word. It was as though he wanted to attract the attention of everyone in the room and was willing to do anything to get it. Which, she knew, was probably exactly the case – as Ben's star had risen, his had fallen. There was no book deal for McConnell. No public adulation. Not even the tabloid papers were interested in him these days. Maybe this was a bid for a second bite of the "cherry of infamy".

"Get out," said Ben, quietly, edging further back, away from McConnell, inching backwards as far as he could. Eventually his back hit the wall and there was nowhere else to go.

Pippa stepped in front of him, shielding him from McConnell.

"I think you'd better leave," she said quietly, trying not to draw attention to what was happening – because that was exactly what he was after. If it all went tits-up, Shelley had more than likely been primed to whip out her phone and get photographic evidence. "He's getting angry and he's got every right to be. And you know what he did to you last time."

"He was just lucky, the bastard!" he said, the fury making him spit his words in her face. "He caught me unprepared. Sucker punched me! And this time, I'm ready – even if he does have his little guard bitch here to protect him!"

He pushed her to the side and she staggered against the wall, looking on in horror as he pranced up to Ben, bouncing on the soles of his feet like a boxer limbering up for the fight.

Pippa looked at Ben, saw his control slipping. Saw his body literally twitching in response to the threat in front of him. Saw his eyes widen and harden as Pippa recovered her balance. Heard him trying to slow his breathing, fighting against his natural urges. She nodded and smiled, letting him know she was fine. That McConnell hadn't hurt her.

If he gave in, she knew, that would be the end of him. Of everything he'd worked so hard to build. Whether McConnell started it or not, Ben would finish it. He was so much bigger, so much stronger. There was no way the other man could win – and neither could Ben. She knew how the violence had eaten away inside him, how his conscience had never rested. How much self-loathing the attack had unleashed. Never mind his book, his career, the publicity – it was his soul that would suffer if he gave in and allowed himself to hurt McConnell again. No matter how much he deserved it.

She saw McConnell wind up, saw him pull his arm back in preparation to take that first punch.

And she ran, straight in front of his fist.

Chapter 18

When she woke up she was in a small room, walls painted uniform white. There were fresh flowers at her side in a vase and the subtle scent of disinfectant that told her she was in a hospital. But, she thought, glancing at the flowers again, a posh one.

She struggled upright, realising as she did it that her head hurt. A lot. She reached up and touched her own face. Yelped as she made contact with swollen flesh and a taped-up nose. Poo. She was channelling Patrick, all those months ago.

It was dark outside, she thought, looking at the window. Nothing but night creeping from the sides of the blinds. The room was set to "night-time" lighting, which meant only one fluorescent strip was glowing over her head. Even that stung her eyes, as if someone was pouring acid onto her retinas.

She blinked it away, moved her head slowly from side to side. The pain was muffled, as though she'd been dosed up with horse pills, but it was there. And it would hurt like hell as soon as the tablets wore off, she knew. She opened and closed her mouth a few times, wincing as it jarred the bruised flesh of her jaw. Ice cream and soup from now on, she thought.

So that, she pondered, was what being punched in the face felt like. Note to self: never do that again.

There was a murmur from the corner of the room, a quiet shuffle, and she realised she wasn't alone. Ben emerged from the shadows, dashing to her side and taking hold of her hand.

He was still dressed in his power clothes, although there was a splotchy red bloodstain on the crisp white of his shirt. The jacket was gone, crumpled up on the back of the chair, and he looked as if he needed a shave. His deep-brown hair was flat on one side and doing the Macarena on the other.

"You look a mess," she said, each word making her cry inside as her lips moved.

"I don't think you're in a position to comment," he replied, smiling gently as he took in her poor, battered face.

McConnell was small, but he'd packed a lot of anger into that punch. Ben would have been able to take it – but Pippa? She was the size of a gnat and the blow had floored her. She'd landed in a heap on the shiny black marble, watching tweety birds and stars flock around her head.

She'd looked up and had seen several Bens dashing towards her. Which, any other time, would have led to some interesting possibilities.

Security guards had piled in as soon as they realised what was happening and McConnell had been dragged away, kicking and swearing, cheated of his prize: another showdown with Ben and the publicity that would follow. Another payday, basically. Instead, all he'd managed to get was a whole heap of trouble – and the reputation for punching small blonde women in the mouth. She'd grabbed hold of one of the Ben's hands, gripping him tightly in case he went after him.

"Don't!" she'd muttered, blood oozing from her split lip. "Leave it – or this will have been for nothing. Then I'll be extremely broomsticked with your molluscs..."

That was the last thing she remembered. Until now. And waking up in a posh hospital room with him by her side. She glanced again at the blood on his shirt. Hoped it wasn't McConnell's.

Ben followed her eyes downwards, saw the state of his own clothes. He gripped her hand even tighter and shook his head.

"No. That's all yours," he said. "You owe me a new shirt."

She tried to smile and his heart almost broke when he saw her wince. He'd had several near-death moments where he'd cradled Pippa in his arms, blood streaming from her nose, completely unconscious. Her body was limp, dead to the world, and her hair smeared in long blonde strands across her bloodied face. He'd wanted, for all the world, to chase McConnell down and smash him to tiny pieces. To crush his windpipe under his boot and tear him apart, limb from crappy limb. But he couldn't – not while she was lying there, like that.

One of the guests, a doctor, had run forward to check her out, while McConnell was hustled away by the security staff to a back room until the police and the ambulance arrived.

The doc had said she was fine, just battered and possibly concussed – but no amount of assurances had helped. Even when the paramedics got there and she was wheeled away on a stretcher, even when he was told she'd regained consciousness, he didn't believe it. He still didn't believe it when the staff at the hospital told him exactly the same. What did they know, after all? It's not as though they were trained medical professionals or anything.

They'd had a fierce job keeping him in the waiting room while they carried out their tests, and it was only when he'd seen himself in a mirror that he really understood why. He was big. He was angry. He was covered in blood. No wonder the nurses were tiptoeing around him. For all they knew, it was him who'd punched her in the face in the first place.

Eventually, they were sure there was no serious damage. Physically, at least. That she just needed some rest, some stitches and some major-league painkillers.

And so he'd sat there in her room, on a chair designed by the Spinal Torture Alliance, for the last four hours. Listening to the quiet beep of the heart monitor. Accosting every nurse who came in to check on her. Watching the gentle rise and fall of her chest as she breathed, grateful to see each inhalation, subconsciously timing his own breath to flow with hers. Eventually, he supposed, he must have fallen into a desperate, restless sleep.

But like a parent alert to the sounds of a newborn, he'd come to when she had, and now they were both awake. Both holding hands. Both battered, in one way or another.

Pippa grunted, considered asking for a mirror, then changed her mind. That could wait. For the time being, it could wait. It's wasn't as though she'd been a supermodel before, and seeing her Frankenstein face would only make her feel worse about the whole situation.

"What's the damage?" she asked instead. "Broken nose?"

"Afraid so, although I'm told it should heal straight. Split lip. Chipped tooth. Bruised cheekbone. You'll have a couple of rugby-player-standard shiners by tomorrow. God, I'm so sorry, Pippa."

"Don't worry," she said, squeezing his hand reassuringly. "Broken noses are something of a family tradition now. I'm just hoping the kids hold out for a few years before getting theirs. Pull up the chair, Ben, you're making me feel tired just looking at you hovering there."

He realised that's exactly what he'd been doing – bent low enough to be near her, but still half-standing, giving him a cramp in his calves he'd never even noticed. Because she was there. She was there, and she was hurt, and she was holding his hand, and she'd saved him from himself by taking the punch that was intended for him. He wouldn't notice it if a parade of naked can-can dancers high-kicked their way around the room.

He did as he was asked and dragged the chair over, positioning it as close as he could without physically sitting on her. Which was what he actually wanted to do, but there were all those annoying wires still hooked up to her arms.

"What happened?" she asked. "After I, you know, did my GI Jane routine?"

"Mainly, you fell over. And bled, a lot. It was...awful."

She heard the strain in his voice, heard what the words weren't quite saying. She imagined how she would have felt, seeing him there like that, not knowing if he was all right or not. Feeling as if it was her fault any of it happened.

"It's okay. I'm okay," she said, quietly. Even now, he thought, even in this situation, she's being the caring one. The kind one. The one who looks after everyone else, even if it involves a slap in the chops and a hospital visit.

She stroked his hand, touching the smooth brown skin, twining her fingers with his. He looked at her, with those chocolate-drop eyes, and tightened his grip. He smiled, raised her hand to his lips, and kissed it, long and slow and caressing, his lips and his tongue flickering over the sensitive flesh of her palm; so familiar, so provocative...

The heart monitor started to beep faster and against the odds they both laughed.

"God, it's good to see you again," he said, keeping her hand snugly between both of his. "And I'd really love to make that thing beep even more, but I can't kiss you properly. Not yet at least. Maybe I shouldn't even be thinking like that, after everything that's happened...looking at you, the kindest thing I could probably do would be to walk away and never see you again."

"And is that what you want to do?" she asked, deliberately keeping her voice as calm as she could. This was his decision. She knew now that she hadn't given up, on him, on her. On them. She still loved him. Had thrown herself in front of a speeding fist for him and probably would do it again. Though she might change her mind about that once the codeine wore off.

She'd come all the way to London to see him, even if it hadn't turned out quite the way either of them had planned. She came all that way to give him another chance – but he had to want it too. And not because he felt guilty, or grateful, but because he loved her, the same way she loved him.

He stared at her, gently swept away the stray hair that was floating across her forehead, tucking it behind her ear.

She could almost see the internal battle being waged and fought to keep her mouth shut, and her heart rate monitor quiet. If she spoke now, she'd never know how he truly felt. If he could love her or if he just felt responsible for her.

"No. It's not what I want to do. I never want to be in a different room from you again," he said, finally, his voice heavy and dark and laden with emotion. "But I've hurt you so much. Much more than McConnell did, I know, even if it looked prettier. I hurt you and I left you. I lied to you and I lied to myself and I walked away. I caused problems with Social Services. I abandoned the kids and then I got you punched in the face. And I hate myself for all of it. I'm terrified that if I don't walk away then I'll hurt you again – and you don't deserve that. You deserve so much better. Better than me, better than this. You told me you loved me and I turned my back on you."

"You did all of that," she agreed, nodding and immediately regretting it as her head throbbed. "But you missed a bit out. On your long list of things you've done."

"What?" he asked, frowning.

"You missed out the bit about making me happier than any man has ever done. The bit about the amazing sex. The bit about the way I always felt so safe with you – so content with you. The way you accepted my family and its weirdness without question. The way you helped Patrick. The way you brought me back to life – gave me back the joy of living that I'd lost when my parents died. The way you filled me up with so much pleasure of every possible kind that I didn't know if I'd ever breathe again without you. Does that count for anything?"

He closed his eyes and when he opened them again there was a distinct sheen of tears.

"It counts for everything," he said, "and I so desperately want to hold you right now. To make you feel safe and happy and content again. To take away all the hurt I've caused and all the damage I've done. But I can't do either of those things. So I'll just say this – I love you, Pippa. I love you with all my heart. I think I did from that very first moment I saw you, waving a toilet brush over your head. But now I understand and I know I shouldn't even ask – but please. Give me another chance. Take me back into your life, into your heart. I'm sorry it took me so long to realise – but I love you, so very much."

She felt a tidal wave of relief food through her, along with the headache and the throbbing pain in her broken nose.

"Well," she finally said, "you are but a man. It's only to be expected that you'd be a bit slow on the uptake. And I do love you, Ben. I never stopped, much as I tried – I just couldn't forget you. But I warn you now – all the complications are still there. I'm still me. You're still you. Social Services will still be involved and the newspapers will still be interested. I love you, but that's not enough. I need to know that you won't leave again. That if you're back, you're back for good. And God, I so wanted to sing that last line in a Take That way..."

"It's the drugs...but Pippa, I am. I am back for good, Pippa, if you'll have me," he said. "Back with you, back with the kids, back fixing the dishwashers. I'll never leave again. As for the rest...we'll overcome it together. We'll make it work. Together."

Epilogue

Barrelstock Bay. A hazily warm June evening. Pippa in her wedding dress and Ben in his suit.

The two of them, alone in the midnight darkness, toasting marshmallows in an illegal campfire on the beach. The only sound that of the waves creeping into the bay, the only light that of the stars in the sky, the sparks from their fire, and the dimmed headlights of the VW van they'd parked up on the cliff to brighten their way down the path.

They'd married in the old chapel at Tregowan Lodge, but abandoned the splendour of the surroundings for a place even more beautiful and even more special.

"I can't believe we snuck out of our own wedding," Pippa said, in between mouthfuls of lip-singingly hot fluff. "That is so naughty."

"Nobody noticed," said Ben, handing her the next sweet on a stick. "They were all too busy drinking the free champagne and dancing. And if anyone does notice, they'll just assume we've gone up to our room for some wedding-night nookie."

"Hmm," said Pippa, grinning at him in the firelight, "and will there be any of that, Mr Retallick? Or are you a bit too tired after all the stress of the day?"

He closed the space between them and threw himself on top of her, pinning her to the ground while she squealed with laughter.

He held her wrists to the sand and straddled her as she pretended to try and get away. In reality, there was nowhere else she'd rather be than here, trapped beneath this big, growling man of hers.

"Stop it," she said, wriggling furiously beneath him, "you're getting my taffeta all creased!"

"It'll be more than creased by the time I'm finished with you, evil witch..." he said, leaning down to shut her up with a kiss.

It was a long kiss and a deep one. One good enough to leave her breathless and fuzzy-headed and a little bit cross-eyed. She could tell from the shape of him pressing through the pretty frock she was wrecking that he'd enjoyed it just as much.

He laughed, rolled onto his back and pulled her head onto his chest. She curled up into his arms, hitching one leg over him possessively. He was hers now. Hers forever. And she was determined to make as much use of him as possible.

It had been a beautiful day, but a tiring one. She'd met Ben's parents for the first time. Had to put on a fancy dress and have her make-up done. Walk through a room full of people in high heels without falling over. And...well, get married. That had been the easiest part – she had no doubts at all about the man she was gazing up at and if she had had any they'd have been chased away by the open adoration in his eyes as they exchanged their vows.

She'd been secretly delighted when Ben had whirled her away from the dance floor and whispered his suggestion in her ear. His fiendish escape plan. They'd go back, eventually, and spend the night at the hotel. Wake up for breakfast with family and friends, before heading off to their official honeymoon in Tuscany.

This, though, was their unofficial honeymoon. Back here, to this special place.

"I still can't believe you never saw it and you came to London anyway," said Ben, laying gentle kisses on her hair. It still smelled of lavender, even if it had been coiffed to within an inch of its life.

"Me neither," she replied, letting her hands sneak up inside his buttoned shirt, fingers creeping over the strong, flat stomach, reaching the muscled ridges of his chest. Sigh. "I guess I'm just a fantastically brave person, aren't I?"

"You are indeed – but I hope you still like the message."

The message in question had been on the first page of his book. The book she'd not looked at in any detail at all once it had fallen out of its packing and into her coffee.

After a few paragraphs of thanks for his agent, his editor and his family, as well as a touching tribute to his grandfather, there'd been one simple dedication: "To Pippa – who found my heart no matter how well I tried to hide it. With love – the Man from the Duck Pond."

If only she hadn't been so freaked out she might have seen it. Might have travelled to London with a spring in her step instead of an anvil in her stomach as she worried about seeing him again.

Still, she thought, smiling as she reached his nipples and made him moan. All's well that ends well. They were here now and everything had been worth it. Even the smack in the face that had resulted in McConnell being the one who went back to jail.

Ben had come back to Cornwall with her as soon as she'd been ready to travel and this time he brought half his life with him. The flat was under offer, the book was launched and there was nothing on earth that was going to keep him away. The kids had been thrilled to have both of them back, and Patrick had given them one raised eyebrow of a look and taken off to see Gemma.

And now they were married. With the full approval of Margaret Dooley, who they'd even invited to the wedding.

"I think," he said, sliding his hand around the front of her dress, "that I'll dedicate my next book to your left breast."

"Oh. Okay," she replied, arching up her body towards his touch. "But the right one might feel left out."

"I'll find a way to make it up to it," he said, lowering his head and showing her how.

Later, after they made love, they lay entangled in each other's arms on the sand, Leonardo's old blanket thrown over them to protect their modesty if a passing spy satellite zoomed overhead. The wedding dress lay creased and sand-strewn next to his suit and her hair was looking less-than princess-like in the moonlight.

She sighed contentedly and snuggled deeper into his arms.

"I love you, Pippa," he said, holding her tighter.

"I know," she replied, kissing the bare skin of his chest.

They lay silently together, basking in the afterglow of both their passion and the now-fizzled-out campfire, listening to the sea whispering towards them.

Pippa looked out towards the bay remembering all the happy times she'd had in exactly this spot. And if she screwed up her eyes and tried really hard she could almost imagine that she saw them there. Her parents. Standing hand in hand on the shoreline, happy and together and smiling.

Smiling at her, the daughter who'd made them so proud. And at the man who held her heart in his hands and cherished it.

The Top Ten Most Romantic Spots in Cornwall

Cornwall is one of the most beautiful spots in Britain – if not the whole wide world! Debbie Johnson certainly fell in love with it, enough to make it the setting for Pippa's Cornish Dream. Here we've teamed up with Visit Cornwall to bring you the ten most romantic spots in the whole of the region. Now all you need to do is find your own Ben Retallick (or your own Ross Poldark of course!), and head south west...

St Nectans Glen Waterfall

This place has all the ingredients for love and romance; ivy clad trees, a sparkling river and the pièce de résistance, a mesmerising waterfall. As you walk hand in hand through the Glen, which has deservedly been bestowed Area of Outstanding Natural Beauty status, you'll sense the waterfall before you actually see it. A feeling of calm, relaxation and togetherness washes over you and this secret hideaway, is the perfect place to share whispered sweet nothings to the serenade of birdsong...just keep an eye out for fairies, piskies and spirits who could be playing gooseberry!
Admission fee applies for visiting the waterfall.
st-nectansglen.co.uk

Porthgwarra Cove

Step into the world of BBC One's much loved Poldark series and head to Porthgwarra Cove in west Cornwall. As the infamous spot where Ross takes a dip in the crystal clear waters while being watched from the cliff tops by Demelza, it is renowned for sending the nation's heart's aflutter. Recreate the lustful scene with a swim of your own or rent the keys to Cosy Cottage which sits in the cove and is a perfect hideaway for loved up couples.

staubynestatesholidays.co.uk/holiday-cottages/

Hot tub sunset at Mawgan Porth

Nothing quite beats the romance of watching the sunset, and in Cornwall you can take your picks of mesmerizing spots to see the sky come alive with the last golden glints of the day. For the ultimate in grown-up indulgence enjoy the spectacle from the warmth of a cliff top hot tub at The Scarlet Hotel in Mawgan Porth. With a glass of something bubbly and your loved one beside you it really is hard to beat.

scarlethotel.co.uk

St Just in Roseland

St Just-in-Roseland Church outside St Mawes has been described as one of the most beautiful churches in the UK and for a small fee you can pay for the church to be lit up at night creating the perfect atmosphere for popping the question. With a magical 'yes' ringing in the air, complete the perfect proposal with a moonlit walk along the beautiful River Fal and take your pick of the Roseland's amazing restaurants and indulgent hotels to celebrate and 'talk weddings' into the small hours.

stjust.roselandchurches.co.uk

Minack Theatre

Pack a picnic and a bottle of something bubbly and cuddle up next to your loved one for an outdoor performance at Cornwall's legendary Minack Theatre, which is carved into the cliff tops above the panorama of beautiful Porthcurno bay. With the stars twinkling above you, a cosy blanket wrapped around you and the stage alive with a plot of passion, lust and romance, it's Cornwall at its most memorable.

minack.com

Lusty Glaze Beach

You could pick any one of Cornwall's beaches and declare them a romantic spot because quite frankly anywhere with glistening sand and crashing waves has the capacity to send couples starry-eyed, but with a name like Lusty Glaze this north coast beach, which is kissing distance from Newquay, has got to be a love highlight. As a unique venue for weddings, the beautiful horseshoe shaped private cove has seen its fair share of romance and for couples that prefer to show their love in less traditional ways, the beach is also renowned for its adventure activities – surely there's no better way to say 'I love you' than on the Lusty 750ft zip wire!

lustyglaze.co.uk

St Michaels Mount

This iconic island has provided the backdrop to countless special moments has been named one of the top places in the country to pop the question, so loved up couples looking for the ultimate in romance can't go wrong by heading to St Michael's Mount. Cross the causeway where a legendary giant once walked, follow the footsteps of pilgrims or boat hop to an island where modern life meets layers of history. Time it right and catch the evocative castle drenched in the glow of a stunning sunset and end your experience with a glass of Cornish bubbly in one of Marazion's many fantastic restaurants that share a picture postcard view of the magical Mount.

stmichaelsmount.co.uk

The Tristan Stone and Fowey

A stone it may be but this isn't just any stone, it is an ancient monument marking the grave of noble Knight of the Round Table, Tristan, who inspired one of the greatest love stories of British history. When Tristan fell in love with the beautiful Irish princess Isolde who was the wife of his uncle, King Mark of Cornwall, it could only be ill-fated and their tragic affair has inspired poets for centuries. So for Valentine dismissive's in need of a helping hand to get into the romantic spirit, this local landmark and its magical tale is a vital pit stop en-route to an intimate meal in Fowey – guaranteed to fill heads with much needed passion!

Frenchman's Creek

Frenchman's Creek on the Helford Estuary was the honeymoon location of choice for Daphne and her husband, Lieutenant-General Frederick Browning. It was here that Du Maurier was inspired to write her novel of the same name about love and pirates. Discover the intimacy and serenity of the area by stepping onto the footpath which runs beside Frenchman's Creek. It is easy to imagine that the call of a waterbird is really the whistle of Daphne du Maurier's French hero, summoning his English mistress to his Breton pirate ship, and that the lapping of the waves is the sound of his first mate rowing in to fetch her.

Drive to Land's End with love

Pretend you're in the movies by taking to the wheel and follow the coastal roads from St Ives to Land's End. With the wind in your hair, smooth tunes on the stereo and views even more beautiful at every twist and turn, it's a drive guaranteed to set the mood for love. The road quite literally hugs the remote coastline and falls away across fields which rest on mighty cliffs making it a journey to go slow and savour.

For more info visit **visitcornwall.com.**

A Q&A with Debbie Johnson

1. Why did you choose Cornwall as the setting for Harte farm?

Like thousands of people before me, as soon as I visited Cornwall I fell in love with it. It's a place that combines wild, rugged beauty with peace and nature and serenity. It's completely magical. My visits to Cornwall have been with children — typical 'are we nearly there yet?' territory – but it still managed to cast its spell. Even on days when there are gale force winds and horizontal rain, it's stunning. I love the clifftop walks, the hidden churches, the riot of colour from all the different flowers. In fact I defy anyone to stand looking down over Tintagel and not be completely mesmerised! So, when I was thinking of a location where I could live out some lovely romantic fantasies, where the surroundings could reflect the emotions, it felt perfect.

2. The Cornish air seems to have worked pretty well for Ben, do you have a favourite place to write?

Yes, my hero Ben – also an author – finds both his muse in Pippa Harte, and in the inspiring surroundings he needs to work on his next book. In real life, I'm more likely to be found in my house in Liverpool – and while we are only minutes away from a beautiful beach, my writing routine is rooted very much in suburbia rather than wild, lush countryside! I did once spend a lovely few days writing outside in the grounds of a farm in Northumberland, right by Hadrian's Wall, which was idyllic but very much the exception!

3. This book is wonderfully reminiscent of English country summers – how did you spend your summer holidays as a child?

I didn't really have childhood holidays, in all honesty. I grew up in Stoke on Trent, which is an industrial city, so it wasn't exactly *Swallows and Amazons*! That said, I do think I probably had more freedom than children seem to today – so I do remember long, hot summers where I'd walk along by canals, or spend hours on end in the park with friends. If we did go away, it was to nearby seaside towns – all very Northern, very fish and chips and donkeys, places like Blackpool and Southport! When I was 19 I moved to Oxford, and the summers there were blissful.

4. Pippa finds a great way to take a break from her responsibilities! What are your favourite ways to relax?

Pippa is a lucky girl – it's only in fiction that a Ben Retallick lands on your doorstep! I love reading. I can completely lose myself in a good book. I'm currently reading Winston Graham's Poldark books and have totally lost my grip on reality! I love movies, music and TV shows, and travelling. I have three kids and two dogs and we spend a lot of time roaming around together, on the beach or in the countryside, and that is a really good way to switch off from the pressures of life that we all face. Also, the occasional night out with my hubby in a city like Liverpool does wonders for the spirits – a good gig, some nice food, and a trawl around all the fab bars and pubs! At least I THINK it does wonders for the spirits...I often can't remember! I have a great group of friends and we all all go to a local pub quiz once a week as well – perfect girl time!

5. Are you a city girl at heart or are you more at home in the country?

I adore visiting the countryside, but I'd have to say city. I love the hustle and bustle and noise and mayhem and sense of history and culture. I love the way you can discover new places even in cities you've been in hundreds of times. I feel quite out of sorts if I can't stick my hand out and hail a black cab! But when I'm organising holidays or breaks, it's usually to the countryside.

6. If you could pick a Prince Charming to check into your holiday lets, who would it be?

Right now, it'd be Ross Poldark. But I am very fickle, and at any given time that could change into James Bond, Sawyer from Lost, Damon Salvatore from The Vampire Diaries, Eric Northman, or Hawkeye from the Avengers. I have eclectic tastes!

7. Do you have any pets and if so, are any of them called SpongeBob?!

Haha! We have two dogs, a Golden Retriever called Toby and a black Lab called Poppy. They're both rescue dogs, so they already had names when we adopted them. Our tortoise, though, was named by us, and is called Rambo — because his shell looks like camouflage gear! So I suppose we are loosely sticking to that theme!

8. What was your favourite thing about writing 'Pippa's Cornish Dream'?

I started it not too long after I'd come home from a trip to North Cornwall, and I loved looking at all the photos from the trip, and allowing my imagination to run a little wild. I enjoyed creating Pippa, who I love – I adore her sense of humour and her strength, and the way she embraces life. It was also something of an enjoyable novelty to write a romance that had quite a few children in it. They always bring an amusing edge to life! I completely lost myself in the story of Ben, Pippa, and the kids, and their life in Cornwall – and I really hope my readers do, too.

Turn the page for a sneak peek at Debbie's #1
Christmas bestseller,
Cold Feet at Christmas

'Fun, sexy and fabulously festive'
Bestselling author Jane Costello

Cold Feet at Christmas

Chapter 1

Jimmy Choo's finest. Pleated white satin. Four inch heels. £500 a pop. For that, you'd expect them to be waterproof, thought Leah Harvey. Or at least to come with jet packs so she could fly out of this godforsaken frozen wasteland, and off to the nearest hotel. Ideally one with a spa, hot and cold running chocolate and Greek god waiters who hand-feed you peeled grapes.

Instead, she was here. In the snow. On Christmas Eve. In the middle of Scottish countryside so remote even the bloody sheep looked like they'd need a sat nav to find their way home.

The lights on the dashboard flickered on and off, casting a final ghostly neon glow before fading into nothingness. She turned the key in the lifeless ignition for the fifteenth time; held her frozen hands in front of the now defunct heating vents, and swore. Long, loud, and with such creative use of foul language that eventually she honked the horn to drown herself out. A self-imposed bleep machine to hide the fact she could make a flotilla of sailors blush.

She undid her seatbelt, noticed that the elegant satin of her ivory dress was now crushed and creased beyond redemption. Not that it mattered. It's not like she'd be using that particular piece of haute couture again.

Climbing out of the cocoon of the car, her feet immediately sank ten inches into freezing cold snow. Her bare shoulders shook with cold, and her fingers and toes decided they weren't even connected to her body as the chill factor took hold. More swearing. This time without the bleep machine. Nearby foxes were probably holding their paws over their cubs' ears.

Great, she thought, turning round to kick the broken-down piece-of-crap car that belonged to her cheating bastard husband-to-be, scuffing the Jimmy Choos in the process. Just great. The perfect end to a perfect day. A gust of icy wind howled up the skirt of her dress, frost nipping at places it had no right to be. Not on the first date, at least. She should be wearing bearskin in weather like this, not a skimpy stretch of silk masquerading as underwear.

She had two choices, Leah decided, teeth chattering loud enough to turn her into a one-woman percussion section. Option One: stay in the car. Wait for help that might never come, as nobody had a clue where she was. Including her. Freeze overnight, and potentially get pecked to death by starving crows she'd be too weak to fight off. The only things left of her would be satin stilettos and her engagement ring.

Option Two: do a Captain Oates and head off across the field to the light she could just about see in the distance. A light must mean habitation, which must mean a human being. Possibly a psychopathic serial killer, or maybe a sex-starved sheep farmer planning Christmas dinner with his collection of blow-up dolls, which, she decided, hitching up the soggy hem of her gown, was still preferable to the crows-pecking-out-eyeballs scenario. She headed for the light.

As she trudged through the fields of snow, she conjured up a playlist of Christmas songs in her head to try and cheer herself up. Or at least help her resist the urge to simply lie down in the ice and sleep. Feed the World. Santa Claus is Coming to Town. Chestnuts Roasting On an Open Fire. Merry Christmas, Everyone... Yeah, right, she thought, slinging her bag over her shoulder and continuing the slow, painful trek to her saviour.

A saviour who probably had one eye, a large collection of shotguns, and slept with his teeth in a jar.

***

Roberto Cavelli had just finished reading a letter from his mother when the knock came at the door.

The contents of the letter didn't surprise him – mommy dearest urging him to move on, remarry and give her the grandchildren she so richly deserved. She'd been telling him the same thing for the last two years, and he'd come no closer to settling down. Plenty to bed, none to wed; which suited him fine. But this time she played all her guilt cards: she was getting older, she'd been so ill, she didn't know if she'd even be here by next Christmas... As *if*, he thought, smiling. Dorothea Cavelli was about as ill as a prize-winning ox in the prime of its life. And she was equally full of bull.

Find a wife, she kept telling him. Pretty much every day, but with special intensity at Christmas, Easter and, her personal favourite, his birthday – because, quote, 'you're not getting any younger, darling'. Since when had 34 been declared officially old? Had there been some kind of United Nations ruling that he'd missed out on? Would he be euthanised at 35 if he hadn't started to procreate? And how come the fact that his twin brother Marco was still playing the field seemed okay with her? He was only an hour younger, for Christ's sake. How come he got a pass on the next-generation nagging?

Well, he didn't want a new wife, thank you very much. He still missed the old one. And even if he *did*, even if he admitted he was starting to feel the slow spread of loneliness creeping across his heart like a silken cobweb, it wasn't that easy. You couldn't just go and buy one from Wives R Us. Well, you probably could, but that wasn't the kind of marriage he'd ever be interested in.

Rob knew that not everyone found love behind every door; and not everyone found their soul mate... definitely not twice. He'd had it once, and he'd let it slip away. Some people just weren't meant to have it, simple as that. And some people – like him – simply didn't deserve it. He'd got used to the idea, learned to function alone, to fake a contentment that he didn't feel. It was over for him. He understood that, and accepted it as part of his fate. His mother, apparently, hadn't. She always had been a stubborn old coot.

So while the letter didn't surprise him – in fact it was depressingly predictable, the way she chased him all over the world to give him a ticking off - the hammering on the door did. He stayed at this cottage for the same two weeks every year. Hiding away for Christmas. Giving himself the greatest gift of all – time away from the sympathetic eyes of his family; from the work that dominated his life; from the ghosts of Christmas past. And during all that time, he'd never once heard a single knock. No visitors, no neighbours, no TV – exactly the way he liked it. Just him, several bottles of very good whiskey, and a suitcase full of books. In fact, when he'd first heard the noise, he'd assumed it was another snowfall – waves of the stuff had been thudding off the roof all night.

When he realised it was actually someone banging on the door to the cottage, he instinctively glanced at his watch. After 11pm. Practically the witching hour out here in the Aberdeenshire wilderness. Man, woman and beast would all be tucked up in bed. Who on earth would be traipsing around in the snow on Christmas Eve? Nobody in their right minds, that's for sure, he thought, walking cautiously towards the door.

Maybe, he thought, as he moved away from the comfort of his spot in front of the fire, it was Santa. With an army of marauding elves. They must have heard about the 50-year-old Glenfiddich he was hiding and formed a raiding party.

Well, he wouldn't go down without a fight. Even to a fat man in a red suit.

***

Please God; please Santa; please Buddha... Please anyone out there who's listening – let there be someone in, prayed Leah. And let them open the bloody door. I don't care if they're evil or have two heads or want to slice me up and eat me with a nice bottle of Chianti. As long as they let me get warm first, I'll go willingly. Anything for a hot drink and a pair of bloody bed socks.

It had taken almost twenty minutes to stagger there, and she knew she was in serious trouble. She couldn't feel anything other than pain: stabbing fingers of cold, all through her body, like daggers of ice. Not just going-clubbing-without-a-jacket cold, but proper this-could-be-your-last-Christmas cold. Real, genuine, get-her-a-tin-foil-blanket-or-she'll-die-of-hypothermia cold. The kind you just never encountered in the city, where there was always a McDonald's to nip into, or a bus shelter full of drunks willing to share their body heat. This was different. And if she'd been capable of thinking straight, she'd have been terrified.

If there was no one in – if the cottage was abandoned, with lights left on to scare off the admittedly unlikely burglars – she was done for. The soul-destroying walk would have been for nothing, and the crows would get her after all. The bastards.

The door finally swung open. She felt tears of relief spring to her eyes, then freeze immediately on her mascara-clumped lashes. She looked up, saw the orange glow of a hissing log fire inside; felt the spill of its light and warmth spreading toward her. Even that tiny lick of heat was enough to make her skin tingle with hope.

Standing right in front of her, silhouetted in the flickering shade and wavering shadows cast by the blaze, was God. Or at least it looked that way to Leah. Surely this creature was too divine to be a mere mortal? Well over six foot; midnight black hair; chocolate drop eyes, a strong jaw just the right side of stubble, wearing a thick cable knit sweater and carrying a glass of whiskey. He certainly looked Almighty enough for her right now.

"Hallelujah..." she muttered, and collapsed into his arms.

***

The last thing Rob expected to see when he opened the door was a woman. No, not just a woman – a bride. A very, very beautiful one at that. Even shaking in her stupidly inappropriate heels she barely scraped five three, but what she lacked in height she made up for in curves. Curves he could clearly see under the satin dress that was soaked onto her like paint; curves that were currently covered in goosebumps; curves that were in fact starting to turn blue. Blonde hair, piled up on her head in a tiara, trailing around her face in tendrils; huge eyes gazing up at him like he was the second coming. Lord, those eyes. The colour of the whiskey in his glass. Pure amber. Lashes tipped by ice flakes; lips parted and shaking as she stared. The Snow Queen looking for her groom.

How on earth had his mother managed this? She was a resourceful woman, but surely even she hadn't been able to deliver a wife for Christmas?

Before he had time to pull a sentence together, the blue-tinged bride on his doorstep muttered one word – he wasn't sure, but it might have been 'Hallelujah' – and fell forward against him. The whiskey glass was knocked from his hand, splashing him with wildly expensive booze and smashing to the floor.

He scooped the woman up into his arms and carried her inside, using one foot to kick the door shut against the howling wind and gusts of icy sleet trying to get in and join the party.

He gently laid her down on the sofa, stroking the melting snow from her cheekbones. She was so pretty…And so cold. Tearing his eyes away from the ample breasts that were now almost peeking out of the strapless satin sheath she was wearing, he grabbed one of the crocheted woollen blankets that were draped on the backs of the furniture, and covered her up. She was in danger of hypothermia. And he was in danger of developing a self-worth problem if he carried on letting his eyes go where they had no right to be. This was not an appropriate time for his libido to come out and play.

He rubbed her hands, leaned over her. Heat. She needed heat. The fire was roaring. The blanket was warm. And he was feeling surprisingly hot himself. Her fingers were like icicles in his grasp, and the breath coming from her lips was still so cold it was clouding into steamy gusts in the air. He edged closer – inches from her face, searching for any kind of response. Suddenly, her lids snapped open, and those amber eyes latched onto his.

He expected to see shock. Fear. Anxiety.

Instead, she murmured 'thank you baby Jesus, Amen'. Kissed him full on the lips. And promptly passed out.

Chapter 2

"Am I dead?" Leah asked almost 16 hours later, when she finally swam back to consciousness.

She'd woken when God walked into the room. He was dressed in faded Levis and a black jersey T-shirt that clung to the muscles of his arms and torso like liquid. He looked suitably celestial, and to top it off was carrying a mug of hot chocolate. With squirty cream on top. For some reason, the words 'squirty cream' and 'torso' blended into one in Leah's brain, resulting in images that were far too vivid to be about God. Positively blasphemous, in fact. If this was Heaven, it had been worth all those years of Sunday school...

She was cocooned in a million tog duvet, her body – naked, which she didn't want to ponder too closely - stretching and writhing beneath the warm fabric, luxuriating in the sensation of soft, cosy heat. Her hair was dry; her fingers had regained a full range of movement, and she could even feel her long-lost toes again. As if that wasn't enough, here he was – her saviour. Sex on a stick and bearing sinful hot beverages. She squeezed her eyes shut, gave her head a shake: Heaven. Must be. The last two days had certainly been enough like purgatory.

"I certainly hope you're not dead," he answered, perching on the side of the bed, long thighs stretching on forever. "Or I wasted a heck of a lot of good whiskey in this mug."

"You're American. I never thought God would be American..." Leah muttered, struggling to sit up straight then realising she had no clothes on and wriggling back down.

"I am," he replied. "American that is. Not God. Although some would say I had delusions of grandeur on that front as well. Glad to see you're feeling well enough to talk. All you did last night and the best part of today was sleep, and sometimes shout about the Hollandaise sauce curdling. Very mysterious. Would it be too much to ask a few questions? Like who you are? And how you ended up here? It's Christmas Day. In the middle of nowhere. And you were definitely dressed for a very different kind of occasion..."

As he finished speaking, Rob saw her eyes flicker over to the hard-backed chair in the corner of the bedroom, take in the fact that her wedding dress, panties, stockings and suspenders were draped over it. He steeled himself for some kind of female hysteria. Because even he – a dumb male of the species — could tell that outfit had presumably been expected to accompany the best day of her life, not one where she nearly died and woke up in a stranger's bed. Buck naked. He'd been trying very hard not to focus on that bit, but as soon as he thought of the words, he felt a familiar twitch in his groin that he knew could embarrass him anytime soon. Should've brought a copy of the paper in with him, ideally a broadsheet.

Leah was quiet for a moment, a small frown marring the milky skin of her forehead as she pieced together the parts of the puzzle. He expected only one possible conclusion: tears, screaming, and possibly physical violence.

Roberto Cavelli took a deep breath in, coiling his muscles ready to run for cover if needed. There was a time to fight, and a time to hide in the broom cupboard, and a wise man knows the difference. Over-emotional women had him sitting on the sweeper every time. He'd leave the cocoa, and run for his life.

Instead, she looked back at him, and smiled. Just like that. A big, gorgeous, open-hearted smile. No shouting. No screaming. No tears. Not even a quivering lower lip. He exhaled, letting out the breath he didn't know he'd been holding. Wow. Maybe she really was from Santa...

"My name's Leah Harvey," she said, sticking her hand out to shake. She kept the rest of her body covered up, managing to awkwardly extend one warm, soft-skinned arm and still look cute. He took her hand in his. It was rude to refuse a handshake, and the Cavelli boys had been raised right.

With the first touch of those soft fingers, he knew he'd made a mistake. He shouldn't be touching this woman at all, even in a hazmat suit. Not with her all warm and curvy, and nude, under those covers. And him with a rapidly developing Crotch Crisis of the first degree. He was going to come across as an utter pervert, damn it.

As her hand clung to his, a tiny spark shot right up his wrist, crawling under his skin like electricity. She felt it too. He could tell by the way she jumped at the sensation. It made the bits of her showing above the duvet jiggle around in a way that did nothing to deter Mr Happy down below. Rob pulled away as quickly as was polite, and crossed his legs.

"Ooh! Did you feel that?" Leah said, giggling and rubbing her wrist. "Must be some kind of weird static thing!"

Yeah. That'd be it, he thought, watching with way too much interest as she manoeuvred herself upright, clutching the sheets in front of her breasts. Her creamy cleavage was mainly hidden by the bedding, but not quite enough to stop a slight spillage of generous flesh over fabric.

Lord, think of something disgusting, he said to himself. Like your brother's sweaty jock strap. Like your 98-year-old Great Aunt Mimi in a bikini. Anything but that killer body in front of you. Not that he hadn't seen it all last night when he'd put her to bed – but that had felt different. That was for medicinal purposes only. He was merely applying correct first aid by stripping her bare of those sodden clothes, that was all. And anyway, he did most of it with the lights off, averting his eyes like a gentleman. None of which had been easy.

"So, what's your name?" she asked, her pink tongue peeking out from between generous lips to lick the cream off the top of her drink. Aunt Mimi, Aunt Mimi, Aunt Mimi.

"Rob," he snapped, sounding a little more terse than he planned. He'd never liked Aunt Mimi. Nasty old coot.

"Okay... Rob. Well, yesterday I was supposed to get married."

"Yeah. My eagle-eyed powers of deduction told me that. Wedding dress and all," he said, nodding towards the now distressed gown hanging limply over the chair back. Leah looked at it and sighed.

"Well, it was supposed to be the whole fairytale deal, you know? Remote Scottish castle. Handsome prince. The only problem was I discovered the handsome prince – Doug — playing hide the sausage with one of the bridesmaids an hour before the service."

"Hide the sausage?" he said, eyebrows raised, slight smile tugging at the corner of his mouth. A mouth, Leah thought, that looked as sinful as his hot beverages. Her eyes lingered on the way his lips curved upwards on one side, like they were asking a question. Wide and full and firm and utterly kissable. Not like Doug's. He had skinny lips. Like his face was so mean it couldn't even spare the flesh. Funny how she'd never noticed that until yesterday. Somehow, seeing him upended in a pile of taffeta had revealed all kinds of little flaws.

"Yes. I'm sure you get the picture. And believe me, he wasn't wearing anything under his kilt either."

"That's... bad. You must be devastated."

Rob stared at her, thinking as he did that she looked the exact opposite of devastated: to him, she looked all silky blonde hair;

wide amber eyes, smiling lips. Lips that were now covered in a cream moustache that he'd dearly like to lick off. There was no sign of impending nervous breakdown, which in itself was off-putting. She'd caught her fiancé cheating; abandoned her wedding, and ended up almost dead on his doorstep – yet seemed calm and content. Maybe he should call the paramedics.

"I know," she said. "It is bad. As bad as it gets. And I should be devastated, shouldn't I? I did what any sane woman would – ran away. Grabbed his car keys and legged it. It was only when the bloody thing broke down across that continent of a field last night I realised I might have been a bit hasty. All I have with me is a bag, a phone with no charger, and some make up. Hence my rather bizarre appearance last night. If I'm honest, Rob, which I always try to be, I ran because I realised I just didn't care.

"It should have broken my heart to see his scrawny little backside pumping up and down on top of Becky, but it didn't. I actually felt nothing but relief. It was like something inside me needed to see it, to make me come to my senses. I didn't want to marry him at all. It was more of a wake-up call than a heartbreak. Plus, you know, the whole almost dying of hypothermia thing – it does put things into perspective. I'm alive. I'm warm. I'm drinking hot chocolate and whiskey – very nice, by the way – none of which I expected to be doing last night."

"Perhaps you're in shock," he suggested. "And you'll start your meltdown any minute now."

She raised an eyebrow, seemed to ponder the idea.

"Yes," she replied. "You could well be right. But don't worry – I'll give you some advance notice if I feel it coming on, and you can make sure you're doing something more attractive, like pulling out your own toenails. Right now, though, I feel quite weirdly calm. I'm worrying about the practical things – what happens next. I work with him. For him, really. We share a home, a car. An iTunes account. Everything. And I left it all behind like it was nothing. The only problem was, my great escape—"

"Landed you here. With a man you don't know. On Christmas Day."

"Yep. Oops-a-daisy. I'm sorry if I've intruded; if I've put you out in any way. And I'm really embarrassed I did a swooner on you as well. Damsel in distress and all that – not usually my style. But I was so cold, and you were so warm."

And gorgeous, Leah continued in her mind. And tall. And hunky. Shoulders so wide they filled the doorframe. Legs so long he could probably leap mountains in a single stride. She could have been hallucinating it all last night, but in the warm light of day, he was even better looking: those velvet brown eyes, completely unreadable. That stubble-coated jaw you could strike a match on. Large hands, wrapped around his own mug, fingers oh-so-long. Denim-clad thighs you could so easily see wrapped around you. He was the sexiest man she'd ever seen, and even looking at him was a sensual feast. She could only imagine what touching would be like. His name might be Rob – but she was sticking with God.

And God, she suddenly noticed, was wearing a wedding ring. In fact, he'd put his mug down and was turning the gold band around and around on his finger, twisting it so hard it must have hurt. Ah. He must have been able to read her mind when she was having inappropriate thoughts about him. Or maybe she'd just dribbled. And now, he was sending her a message: back off, taken man.

Received, understood, and undoubtedly for the best, she decided. She was insane to even be thinking of him in that light – right now she should have been starting life as Mrs Anderson, on honeymoon in St Lucia. Instead she was eyeing up tall, dark and gorgeous here, and wondering if he fancied slipping under the duvet for a quick game of tonsil tennis. Maybe she'd taken a bang to the head when she collapsed. Maybe she was experiencing some weird kind of frost-related hormone rush. Maybe she had an undiagnosed multiple personality disorder and would start speaking in fluent Finnish any minute now.

He wasn't even her usual type. Way too big and broad and dark and foreign and sexy. For God's sake, what woman in her right mind would fancy that? She suppressed a giggle, and started to wonder if the concussion angle might be real. She couldn't ever remember having this kind of physical response to a strange man before. In fact, to any man at all. It was completely out of character, but nobody seemed to have told her body that. Her body was convinced that he was its very best friend, and was getting all warm and squishy to prove it.

Even though he was now practically scowling at her, she still had the urge to reach out and touch his jawline, run her fingernails over the stubble and see if it prickled; to trace the bold outline of those lips with her tongue... MARRIED, she shouted at herself. Silently. Even if her body had lost all moral fibre, she wasn't going to start ravishing married men. He could still be a serial killer anyway, even if he did have the looks of a slightly fallen angel.

The way he was looking at her right now, for example, was unsettling. There was quite a lot of Leah on show, she realised, which didn't bother her. She had no problems with body image, and could count her inhibitions on one hand. But his eyes were so dark; his pupils large and black and focused so intensely on hers that she started to feel breathless. Neither of them was speaking, but the air between them seemed to sing, to thrum with some kind of energy. Even the expression on his chiselled face was creating a throbbing pulse between her legs. If someone lit a match, the room would go kaboom, there was so much spark.

"Don't worry about it," he said finally, his voice clipped and short and tense. For a moment she couldn't recall what she'd even said. Oh yes. An apology for disturbing him. Swooning on him. Drooling on him. Fantasising about him.

"There are women's clothes in the wardrobe," he snapped. "I think you'll be way too big for them, though. If you are you'll have to use something of mine."

Right, Leah thought, nodding and smiling as best she could. Thanks a million, mate. That comment definitely slowed the pulse rate down a beat or two: nothing like being called a heifer by an attractive man to kill the mood. She knew she was more voluptuous than was fashionable these days, but she'd never had hang-ups. Men seemed to like it, too. Doug certainly had, until he'd decided he preferred the bridesmaid. But after those marvellously chosen words from Rob, she felt about as feminine as a prop forward for the England rugby team. Too big for women's clothes. Wear something of his. Surely the fool realised that his clothes would swamp her, D-cups notwithstanding? Stupid idiot man.

This particular stupid idiot man seemed to realise he'd said something wrong, as he frowned, glowered, and stood up abruptly. He marched out of the room, absently running his hands through his hair and murmuring something about needing to chop down some trees. He was still muttering as the door slammed shut behind him.

Okay, thought Leah, scampering out of bed and darting through the chilly air to the wardrobe. Weird situation, but deal with it. So he's moody. Probably some eccentric artist type, holed up here in a stone cottage on his own for Christmas. Without his wife... What kind of a wife would let a man like that out of her sight for any length of time anyway?

None of your business, she reminded herself firmly, holding up a pair of jeans that would never in a million years fit her. Surely they were made for a child, not a full-grown woman? No way her hips and bottom would shoehorn themselves into that thimble-full of denim. He must be married to a midget. Okay, that wasn't fair. Speaking as a woman who only topped five foot on a big hair day, Leah knew there was nothing wrong with being vertically challenged.

But this midget must also be really skinny. The kind who made a single pomegranate seed last all day, with one low-fat raisin for pudding. The bitch.

She had better luck with a pair of stretchy leggings, and a plain long-sleeved white T-shirt. Admittedly it looked like it was sprayed on, and there was no bra anywhere near her size. The wedding dress had some kind of industrial strength cantilever device built in, robust enough to support the Forth Bridge, never mind her boobs.

Now she had nothing, unless she wanted to wander round like Miss Haversham all day, in a dirty, torn bridal gown. Yet another genius move on her part. If only she'd known she'd be doing a runner from her own wedding, she'd have packed an overnight bag. She'd kill for her own knickers right now.

She turned and stared into the mirror, examining her ensemble. Oh well, she thought, I am most definitely a beggar, and therefore can't afford to be a chooser. And anyway, you can't *really* see my nipples. Not unless you look really hard. Or they start to misbehave in the cold. She tugged and pulled at her hair, trying to dislodge some of the dried-on product that had moulded it around her tiara, and decided that was as good as it was going to get.

"Hey, Rob?" she shouted as she emerged back into the living area. "Are you still in here? Are you chopping down trees, and if not, can I use your phone? Mine's out of juice and I really need to organise getting out of here."

Getting out of here and getting home as quickly as possible, she decided, was today's mission impossible. Yesterday's had been escape, and later survival. Now she had to move on. To London. To their flat. To get whatever she needed and leave, before she had to face Doug again. To disappear to Timbuktu. Take a midnight train to Georgia. Join a commune in Marrakesh. Become a nun – if they took nuns in when they were 25. Whatever it took to save her dignity and spare them both the useless recriminations. Some relationships simply weren't fixable. Funny how she'd not even admitted to herself it was broken until yesterday. Years of limping along, so used to the problems that they'd become normal. That would hurt at some point, she knew, but not now. Now she needed to be practical.

"There's no signal here," Rob said, emerging from the kitchen, holding a tea towel. He'd obviously decided to dry the dishes before he went logging. He stopped dead in front of her, and stared like she'd grown a third eye.

"What?" she said, feeling alarmed. "What's wrong?"

"That... that top."

"Oh! That. I know. You were right about the clothes. It doesn't really fit, does it?"

"No," he replied, still staring. "You're more..." he trailed off, making vague body-shape gestures in the air with his hands.

"More what?" she asked. Voice quiet. Hands on hips. Eyes narrowed. Oh-oh, Rob thought, recognising that tone. Danger, danger. Tread carefully, lost soul, or you may never pee straight again.

"More... womanly?" he said, looking at her cautiously, one eyebrow raised in a question. She nodded, seemed happy enough with that, thank God. He came here every year for peace and quiet, and he could do without a cat fight with someone he barely knew to bring in the festive season.

Although, he thought, taking another look at that T-shirt and what jiggled beneath, there were some parts of her he was getting to know quite well already. Maybe he'd become immune with repeated exposure, like with flu or chicken pox. Or maybe, a faint stirring in his nether regions told him, not.

"I can see your nipples through that material," he said, dragging his eyes away. "I think that's probably illegal. And if not, it should be."

"Oh," she replied, looking down at her own chest, realising that even his glance had made the nipples in question do some quite embarrassing things. She looked back up, blushing. "I didn't think you could see unless you looked really really hard."

"In case you hadn't noticed, I'm a man," he said. "And it's in our nature to always look at these things really really hard."

Leah laughed out loud, throwing her head back so the creamy skin of her throat was exposed.

Rob, being still male, couldn't help but notice the way the movement made her breasts jut out just a fraction more as she filled her lungs with air and giggled. He wanted to pull that skin-tight T-shirt up, and bury his face in them. Lord, how was he expected to resist her? Should he even try? Where had this sudden attack of morality come from anyway? Must be a Christmas thing. He'd been infected with goodness. Hopefully it was only temporary. He was only flesh and blood, after all.

"I *had* actually noticed you're a man," she said, liquid amber eyes running over his body, taking a lazy inventory of what she saw. Slowly she looked him up and down: legs that seemed as long as her whole body; Levis clinging low to his hips; the curved ridge of pectoral muscles evident through the jersey top. Powerful shoulders, biceps that flexed even as she looked... Gosh, he was an absolute treat. She stared, licked her lips, and filed the image away in her brain. Under S for Sexbomb.

He might be married, but that hadn't made her blind. She couldn't be the only woman who noticed how handsome he was, and anyway, there was no harm in window shopping. Look, but don't touch: the same theory she had for the Stella McCartney shop in Selfridges. Except, in this case, it was harder to resist. She couldn't help wondering if those biceps were as firm as they looked, if that chest was as hard and sculpted as it seemed under the long-sleeved T; how that backside would feel snuggled into the grip of her hands. Whether the tell-tale bulge she could see in his jeans was as promising as the ever-tightening denim suggested. Her